WILSON

Jack Finn

Crow Street Press

Copyright © 2025 Jack Finn

All rights reserved

The characters and events portrayed in this book are fictitious. Any similarity to real persons, living or dead, is coincidental and not intended by the author.

No part of this book may be reproduced, or stored in a retrieval system, or transmitted in any form or by any means, electronic, mechanical, photocopying, recording, or otherwise, without express written permission of the publisher.

ISBN-13: 979-8310238671
ISBN-13: 979-8266550391

Cover design by: Blaine Daigle
Contact Jack Finn for Library of Congress Control Number
Printed in the United States of America

For Roxana, my inspiration for all things great and small.

CHAPTER 1

The crow glided above the field of parked cars and pickup trucks, the grass brown and dry from the summer sun. He watched as the people below made their way up the steep rise from the vehicles toward the carnival's gate, eager to get inside. They reminded him of so many ants milling about their nest.

From a copse of trees beyond the parking lot, a pair of crows rose up to intercept him, their black eyes staring at the interloper, the trespasser, within their domain. One cawed in warning; crows were notoriously territorial and the newcomer was most certainly not welcome.

The crow answered back menacingly, a deep throaty sound, and dove at the pair. He angled away from the sun so they could see his body, marked and scarred from dozens of past challenges. His caw was an unrepentant war cry, laced with the promise of blood and pain. The sound chilled the other two birds to their cores, sapping their courage. They had the numbers, but he had the will to fight, and no mere show of force would deter him. As one, the two crows turned, cawing their capitulation as they fled.

He gave chase, noting the desperate flapping of their

wings to gain speed, but then slowed. Catching up to the pair would be easy for him, but he had no desire for that; the rest of the murder would receive the message to steer clear of the newcomer without the need for bloodshed. These crows eked out an existence off carrion and what could be gathered in dry, withered farm fields. The arrival of the carnival was a boon for them, as for a short time they could dine upon the culinary flotsam and jetsam of the patrons.

However, that was not the lot in life for this crow; he followed the carnival as they made their way from one town to the next—ever since the procession had turned West down the panhandle toward New Mexico, though that was a name he did not know. The crow knew only that to the West lay home and his roost beneath the cool lip of the canyon.

His coal black eyes watched the two crows careen to the south and flee back to the safety of their murder, the black bodies of the others dotting the tree branches. The challenge averted, the crow veered back toward the south side of the carnival, his eyes locking on his original destination—the small, gray tent.

If there was one thing the crow did not like about the carnival, it was the man in the bland, gray tent; the man smelled wrong. He had the odor of something putrid and foul, like the stench of carrion but different in a way the crow did not understand. The crow did not like the man and the man's malfeasance did not go unnoticed.

However, the crow was a crow and the man was a man, so there was little he could do but watch. He once caught the man glancing askew at him with such malevolence in his gaze that the crow knew the man despised him, though whether his scorn was directed at the bird personally or all of his kind the crow did not know.

As the crow's feet landed soundlessly on the gray tent, the bird thought back on the day the man had struck him with a rock. He had been watching a pickpocket in the crowd, when it had struck him painfully upon the back. Had the rock been bigger or the blow harder, say upon his head, it could have caused serious injury. The crow had glimpsed the leering smile of the man as he flew off.

That afternoon the crow waited for the man to walk amongst the throng of carnival goers and then swooped down and shat upon him. The gooey wad struck the shoulder of the man's black coat and splattered across his cheek. The crow saw the enraged man wiping at the side of his face as he glared upward into the sky. Passersby in the crowd gasped and snickered at the voluminous amount of bird waste that had been deposited on the man.

Now, with utmost care, the crow hopped across the canvas roof of the gray tent. The hole was small, only a little larger than a thumbnail, as the crow peered down at the sleeping form of the man. He was certain that when the rains came again the man's bed would be drenched.

The crow dipped its head and plucked at the tough canvas strings with his beak, pecking and pulling to expand the hole.

***

Wilson's eyes snapped open. Light streamed through the small hole in the roof of his tent, the sun's rays dancing across his face as his thin body lay on the sweat-stained cot. His ragged blanket must have slipped off during the night, and as he sat up, the narrow band of sunlight cast a line across his body, from his dingy white underwear up across his hairless, sunken chest to glint off the small iron key he wore on a thin wire around his neck.

He glanced up at the hole in the tent and spied something moving besides the opening, its shadowy shape outlined by the sun as it tugged at the exposed threads. A bird was tearing at the tent.

The thought of the bird damaging his tent enraged him. Snatching a half-eaten apple from his night table, Wilson hurled it upward. The apple thumped loudly against the canvas rooftop, close enough to dislodge the bird. He could hear the bird cawing loudly as it flapped away.

A crow! Fucking flying rats, that's what they are.

Wilson sucked air in through his nose and blew it out his mouth, a breathing technique one of his late uncle's many girlfriends had taught him to calm his anger when he was a child.

"Smell the flower, blow out the candle," she used to tell him.

The hot, sticky air bore the scent of stale popcorn and cotton candy. Wilson frowned. Judging from the number of voices passing his tent, the carnival had opened for the day. He must have slept late.

How unlike me. Hamish will be furious if I don't have the photo booth open with the carnival so newly arrived in whatever shithole Oklahoma Panhandle town this is.

He stood and stretched. Though only in his late thirties, his spindly arms and legs crackled and popped like burning firewood as he shook off the night's slumber. He surveyed the tent as he blinked the sleep from his eyes. It contained all he owned in this world: the old cot, a standing coat rack with his rumpled black suit and ragged top hat hanging from its lone hook, a vertical mirror, a small table with a tin pitcher of water and a chipped drinking glass, and a rusty lantern that hung on the tent pole. His gaze drifted toward the locked wooden trunk across from his bed, ensuring the heavy iron lock sat closed securely just as he had left it.

All safe and sound.

He smiled as his eyes lingered on the chest, then glanced sidelong at the elongated oval cheval mirror. Its dark wooden frame, decorated with foliate carving following the form of the mirror, sat seated between two tapering uprights, finished with a pair of intricately carved finials. The mirror was held in place by a smooth, tarnished brass knob on the side of each upright, which allowed it to be adjusted to tilt for a full-body reflection. The mirror's curved bracketed feet, fashioned to resemble lion paws, dug snuggly into the dusty Midwestern earth. Wilson had discovered a fading stamp on the back of the mirror that read "Morrison & Co. of Edinburgh"; he surmised it must have started its life Scotland and often wondered if all the mirrors there were so intricately carved.

How it had made its way across the Atlantic to America was a mystery to Wilson. It had once belonged to a vaudevillian performer who had joined the carnival as a juggler.

"A good mirror is the mark of an important man, Wilson, and this is an exceptional mirror," the man had said.

"What makes it so exceptional?" Wilson asked.

"If you're searching for the person who will change

your life, look in the mirror. Exceptional mirror, exceptional person."

Wilson thought there was nothing exceptional about the man, but from that moment on, he had coveted the mirror. He wanted to see himself in that mirror, to be exceptional too.

The rotund man had died atop one of the working girls in the midst of carnal relations. Wilson had heard the woman's cries for help as she struggled to get the man's bulk off of her. As several workers rushed to her aid, Wilson had slipped into the man's tent and took the mirror. It was not stealing. The man was dead after all and it would not be long before the other residents of the south side came to rummage through his other possessions and claim anything of value.

Grabbing the black suit from the coat rack and throwing it on the bed, his thoughts drifting back to Hamish's expected anger at his tardiness.

"Can't blame a man for sleeping," he grumbled.

Wilson buttoned up the white shirt; its collar, yellowing from use. He pulled on the baggy, black pants and jacket. Reaching into the jacket's pocket, he produced a red clip-on bow tie and secured it to the collar of his shirt. He reached up and swiped the few remaining greasy wisps of dark hair across his balding scalp before placing the well-worn top hat on his head.

Only once he was fully dressed did he kneel before the wooden trunk and run his bony hands over the cherry wood top. The trunk was worn, scratched, and dinged, but it held all his treasures. His eyes darted around the room, looking for any prying eyes before reaching into his shirt and producing the small metal key. He leaned down and unlocked the trunk's heavy iron lock, without removing the wire from around his neck, then slipped the key back inside his shirt.

He then opened the lid and peered down into the trunk. A dark blanket secreted all his treasures from view, all except his camera, which he lovingly picked up. It was of simple construction. A rectangular leather box with a circular lens eye at its front was positioned just above the narrow slot that produced the pictures. There was a square viewport on top that you looked down into to frame your shot, a small brass winding handle on the side, and two levers, one above the other that independently operated the shutter. There was a leather hand strap secured to the top of the box to carry the camera, but Wilson never used it. He kept it clutched against his body when he walked, secure against thieves and anyone who could bump into the camera and damage it.

Wilson could see his reflection in the camera lens: his dark sunken eyes and thin, pointed nose. He smiled with a mouth full of yellow-stained teeth and cradled the device in the crook of his arm.

His hand reached up to close the lid, then paused and drifted down to caress the dark blanket. His treasures were underneath, just beneath the blanket, and hhe felt a euphoric rush at the thought of them so close to his touch. The thought aroused him, and he licked his lips, barely containing the desire to pull the blanket away, his fingers trembling with longing.

Maybe just a little look.

He nodded his head. Yes, that would be alright. Just a

look.

No tasting, just a look.

He shook his head. He would just look, not taste. His memory rolled back to the taste, and his eyes nearly rolled back in his head in ecstasy.

Maybe just a little taste.

A lascivious grin spread across his face at the thought, but the screeching cry of a child outside snapped him from his reverie. The noise of the carnival was growing noticeably outside. He needed to get going.

"People should keep their fucking children quiet," he growled, gritting his teeth in frustration.

With a sigh, he closed the trunk and slid the heavy lock into place, tugging it three times to make sure it was locked securely. He then walked over to stand in front of the mirror and studied his reflection. It struck him how much he looked like his late uncle, increasingly so as the years passed. They had the same slight frame, sallow complexion, and thinning hair, so unlike the robust, broad-shouldered frame of his father.

He smiled as he looked at the reflection of his beloved camera, nestled in the crook of his arm. The black suit hung ill-fittingly over his small frame and rounded shoulders, and the red bow tie hung precariously from the collar of a shirt too loose for his thin neck. He peered out from beneath the brim of a top hat constantly threatening to sink over his eyes. Wilson rubbed a hand over the pale skin of his jaw and sunken cheek bones, noting the smoothness of his skin. No shave needed today.

"Don't we look fine today?" He grinned into the mirror.

"Yes. Yes, we do."

CHAPTER 2

The Grand Ole Traveling Carnival was a veritable roving city of tents that made its way through the dustbowl of the American Midwest, setting up in a new city for two weeks each month.

"One week is divine, two weeks is grand, but three is too long," Hamish White, the carnival's proprietor and ringmaster, was fond of saying.

They would spend the winter on the West Coast before making their way back across America the following year to winter in the Florida panhandle; then the cycle would start again, crisscrossing America.

The north side of the carnival was home to the big tents where the animal shows, performers, and grand carnival spectacles took place. All manner of food could be found there, from savory meats to sweet cotton candy. This was where the families went, with wide-eyed children screaming in delight.

But the south side of the carnival was a different world. The tents of the south side were smaller and more intriguing places where only the more adventurous townsfolk would come seeking freak shows, tattoos parlors, or to watch private fighting matches between men or animals. Some came seeking drugs or the services of some of the ladies of ill repute that traveled with the carnival.

Wilson squinted as he stepped out of his tent into the bright daylight; the sights and sounds of the carnival assailed his senses. He rarely went to the north side of the carnival. There were too many people bumping and jostling; they would break his camera if they got too close with their pushing and shoving. But on the south side, people moved more slowly: talking in hushed tones, peering in open tents, or talking with the carnival barkers, who tried to lure passersby into their secretive world of delights and oddities.

He skulked about the fringes of the line of tents, needing to get to his photo booth before Hamish saw him.

"Running late again, Wilson?" called a man with a thick Chinese accent.

"Hamish will feed you to the bears if you're late, Wilson!" laughed a deep male voice.

"What could a bear eat? He's just skin and bones!" said the Chinese-accented voice.

"I never see you eat, Wilson. You need to put some meat on those bones," the other voice mocked.

Wilson cringed at the sound of the two familiar voices and turned to sneer at their source, two of the south side's more popular attractions. The Chinese voice belonged to Long Li, a tall, thin Chinese man with a neck that was over two feet long, earning him the moniker of Long Li, the Giraffe Man of Shanghai. Wilson often thought that the man's head looked so precariously perched atop his long neck that it could come tumbling off at any moment. Li would amaze carnival goers by swallowing oddly shaped objects they would then watch travel down his long neck. They would then be delighted to watch the objects travel back up his neck and out his mouth. The carnival goers loved it, but Wilson thought it was quite disgusting.

The other man was The Human Walrus. Wilson knew that was not the name his parents gave him at birth, but he never really bothered long enough with the man to learn his real name. The Human Walrus was a heavyset man with dark, bushy hair and a large mustache, who Wilson admitted closely resembled the painted walrus on the carnival poster. But his most startling features were his two obscenely long canine teeth extending past his chin. At the carnival, the man earned his keep by popping balloons, skewering fruit, and poking holes in cans with his two large teeth. He was always very popular with teenage boys, who seemed to delight in throwing fruit at the large man and watching him spear it midair. Wilson supposed that one day, those long canines would snap off on some hard can or unripe fruit and the man would no longer be useful to Hamish.

Hamish had brought both men back from a trip to San Francisco last summer and now the two shared a tent on the edge of the south side. Wilson knew they were constant gossipers, and if they saw that he was late setting up his booth, half the carnival would know shortly. He hurried past the two men and headed into the space that divided the north side of the carnival from the south side. His little booth sat in the middle of the open space.

As he approached the small booth, he felt someone come up alongside him, a teenage boy scampering on all fours. The boy wore overalls with a lion-like tail sewn onto the back. He looked up at Wilson with light blue eyes that peered out of an adolescent face ringed with a mane of dirty brown hair that ran from the top of his head around his face. The boy had used black paint to darken his nose to make it look more lion-like.

"Wilson," the Lion Boy ran alongside him on his hands and feet, "Hamish has been looking for you."

"Thank you, Henry." Wilson winced, noticing several young children pointing at the Lion Boy loping alongside him. He did not need any added attention this morning.

"He's very annoyed, Wilson. He's been looking for you all morning."

"Thank you, Henry. You should run along." Wilson made a shooing gesture with his hands for the boy to hurry off.

Henry gave Wilson a hurt look. It was not so much that Wilson disliked Henry; in truth, he had no opinion of him whatsoever. The boy was billed as half boy, half lion, and would perform for the crowd before the real lions came out in the big tent. Wilson had watched the boy's act once as he jumped through a flaming hoop and caught raw pieces of meat out of the air.

"Have it your way." The Lion Boy veered off from Wilson to head towards a group of men and women.

Wilson saw the boy stop behind two women and roar like a lion at the group; the women yelled in surprise, clutching their hands to their breasts in mock terror, then joined the rest of the group clapping in appreciation as they watched Henry scamper off to the next crowd.

When Wilson reached his little booth, he noted the morning crowds were still relatively sparse, and it would be at least another hour or so before the carnival would start to fill with the day's customers. The sign over the booth announced "Hamish White's Phantasmagorical Photos!" with a small, round placard that read "25 cents" just below the counter where Wilson sat on his uncomfortable wooden stool. The sign irked him to no end.

It should read Wilson's Phantasmagorical Photos.

He often thought about this. It was his camera and he took the pictures after all.

He was thankful that at least the booth had a wooden ceiling that kept the hot Oklahoma sun from beating down on him. Wilson took his place on the wooden stool and withdrew a handkerchief from his pocket, lovingly wiping down the camera. He swirled the soft cloth over the delicate glass lens, the shiny metal winding handle, and the leather-skinned frame. He was always careful not to accidentally press the shutter-release, the lever that sat next to the winding mechanism that advanced the film while he cleaned. That would waste film. And never the lever below it.

Well… not never.

Wilson smiled at the thought of the times his finger rested atop the cool metal of the lower lever and applied pressure. A shadow passed overhead, and the smile slipped from his face as he leaned out of the booth and spied a crow circling the sky above.

Another fucking rat with wings.

His hand gravitated to the spot on his shoulder, where the bird's filth had landed earlier. He had scrubbed at the spot until the threads began to fray to be sure the creature's vile excrement was completely gone. Wilson was so consumed with glowering at the crow that he failed to notice the two people approaching his booth.

"Hello there. We'd like to have our picture taken," a smiling bald man said, walking up to the booth with a young boy.

Wilson looked up at the pair. The man was tall and lean with a drab shirt and pants that seemed so typical of the people in these towns, but the boy with him wore a bright white sailor suit and sported an unruly head of dark curly hair.

"Of course. That will be twenty-five cents, please," Wilson gave the man a wide smile that he had practiced in the mirror. Hamish chastised him repeatedly that he needed to have a more welcoming smile, one that made people want to say 'please take my money.'

The man handed Wilson several small coins, which he slipped through an open slit carved in the top of the counter, making a loud clinking noise as they dropped into the locked tin box beneath. Wilson stepped out of the booth and positioned the two so that one of the carnival's large red tents stood behind them.

He looked down into the viewport. "Now, just give me a nice smile."

As he looked through the viewing hole of the camera, the man placed his arm on the boy's shoulder and grinned widely. However, Wilson's attention went to the figure he spied over the man's shoulder.

Hamish White was headed straight for Wilson's booth with his unmistakable red pants and jacket, bright white shirt, and black top hat. The carnival owner's suit and hat always looked impeccably clean, his black boots were always perfectly shined, and all of it fit as if it was tailored specifically for him. Alongside him was a thin, stiffly walking woman in a dark gray dress running from her neck to her ankles.

"Did you take the picture?" The bald man's question snapped Wilson out of his momentary distraction.

"Just one more moment."

He ensured the smiling man and his son stood framed correctly in the shot. He then lightly depressed the shutter release, the camera made a loud click, and t began making a whirring noise. A black square slid out of the picture slot, and the man and his son gathered around to take a look. As Wilson stared at the black picture, the image of the man and his son slowly began to take shape, the large carnival tent silhouetted against the sun behind them. Wilson's eyes kept darting to the side, watching the approaching form of Hamish and the woman.

"Hmph." The bald man frowned, looking down at the picture.

Wilson looked back down at the picture. The details were much clearer now, and he could see that the man had closed his eyes as the camera snapped the picture. The boy, too, had glanced up as if looking at a bird just as the camera captured his image.

"What a fine pair you make," Wilson offered as he handed the man the photograph.

"Let me see, Father." The boy plucked the picture out of Wilson's hand.

The man continued to frown and appeared ready to ask Wilson for another picture, when the boy laughed loudly.

"Father, you look so funny!" he laughed, his face a visage of pure delight.

Seeing his son's pleasure, the man's expression softened, and he nodded to Wilson. They turned to leave just as Hamish and the woman arrived.

Hamish was a tall man, which was further accentuated by his high black top hat. The man's pale white complexion contrasted with his jet-black hair and thin mustache that, of course, perfectly traced his upper lip. Wilson never liked looking anyone directly in the eye, and he found Hamish's piercing stare, with his hazel eyes that flashed golden yellow like a coyote's in the sunlight, like the coyotes that sometimes lurked at the fringes of the carnival at night, to be particularly unsettling. He avoided holding the man's gaze at any cost.

"Wilson, so good to finally find you!" Hamish gave a toothy smile.

"Good to see you too, Hamish." Wilson took out his handkerchief and pretended to clean the camera's lens again.

Hamish gestured to the woman standing beside him. "Wilson, I wanted to introduce you to our guest."

Wilson looked at the woman glancing around the carnival with a look of distaste on her face. Her grey hair sat in a tight bun, and she appeared to have a face turned into a permanent scowl as if she constantly sucked on sour lemons. She had small, cold, dispassionate blue eyes that looked to be judging the world harshly from behind the round spectacles perched on her pointed nose. The woman clutched a bible and her black handbag with both hands against her chest as if expecting a purse snatcher to come running out of the crowd at any moment.

"Wilson, this is Mrs. Stammerall from the Council on Family..." Hamish started before appearing to search his memory for the words.

"From the Council on the Protection of Family Values and Proper Behavior," Mrs. Stammerall added, giving Hamish a withering stare.

"Yes. Yes, that's it." Hamish clapped his hands together and grinned.

"Nice to meet you." Wilson felt as uncomfortable beneath the woman's stern gaze as he was with Hamish's.

"Wilson, Mrs. Stammerall has some concerns about our good carnival," Hamish said, feigning a hurt tone.

"To be exact," Mrs. Stammerall further straightened her already stiff posture, "the C.P.F.V.P.B. has concerns that your carnival does not conform to the standards of decency that we have set for the good people of our town. We have heard reports of drunkenness, lewd acts, fighting, and all manner of immorality taking place here, Mr. White. Not to mention that your carnival is open on Sunday, which is the Lord's Day; it is not a day for the people of this town to be tempted by your traveling den of debauchery."

Hamish gasped and placed his hand over his heart in faux pain. "I assure you the Grand Ole Traveling Carnival is no such place, Mrs. Stammerall. If the P.V.C.S.B..."

"The C.P.F.V.P.B.," she corrected. "As President of the Ladies Committee of the C.P.F.V.P.B., I will meet with Mayor Anders to demand he shut your carnival down immediately."

"Mrs. Stammerall," Hamish's tone was soothing, "that is why I brought you to meet Wilson here."

Me?

Wilson failed to hide his astonishment.

"Let me at least make a peace offering," offered Hamish, extending his hands in a humble gesture.

"Hmpf," snorted Mrs. Stammerall. "I need nothing from the wages of sin."

"Oh, of course not, Mrs. Stammerall. Wilson is just a photographer. I simply wanted to offer you a picture to remember your day at the carnival."

Wilson held up the camera to show her and watched as her cold blue eyes studied the leather and chrome camera for a moment. Then, he detected the faintest hint of a smile cross her face. He knew that in her mind she saw the C.P.F.V.P.B. using the picture in a local paper under a headline that would read something along the lines of "C.P.F.V.P.B. Defends Town's Morals and Closes Carnival."

"Well, a picture would be nice, Mr. White," she said, her voice taking on a conciliatory tone.

"I am happy you agree!" grinned Hamish

Mrs. Stammerall smoothed out the wrinkles on her gray dress and touched her tight hair bun to ensure it was firmly in place. She stood ramrod straight and offered a tight-lipped smile of determination as Wilson looked down into the viewport. He angled it to center her in the camera's frame before moving his finger to the shutter release.

"Wilson," Hamish hissed through his smile, "I think you

meant to press the shutter release on the bottom."

"On the bottom?" Wilson looked at him questioningly, his cheeks twitching as he felt a feral joy course through his veins. He caught sight of the look in Hamish's eyes, briefly changing from hazel to golden yellow, and looked back into the viewport as a wolfish grin crossed his face. "Yes, of course, the shutter release. How foolish of me."

He stared through the viewport at the sour-faced woman, rigidly holding her bible, and slowly depressed the lower lever. Just as it had done earlier, the camera made a loud click and then a whirring noise. A darkened square slid out of the picture slot and Wilson handed it to Mrs. Stammerall.

"Free of charge, of course," added Hamish.

As Mrs. Stammerall stared down at the dark image, Hamish held his hands behind his back and began to whistle a jaunty tune. The woman looked up at him disapprovingly, and Hamish gave her a wide grin, pointing for her to continue watching the photo develop.

Mrs. Stammerall peered at the picture dispassionately as the blackness slowly gave way to greater detail. She then gasped loudly and clutched her bible to her chest as she looked at the picture.

"Is there something wrong, Mrs. Stammerall?" Hamish peeked over at the picture. "Why, Mrs. Stammerall, you look positively radiant!"

"How? How is this possible?" Mrs. Stammerall stared from the photo to Hamish.

She held out the picture. Standing amidst the tents and crowds of the carnival stood Mrs. Stammerall, but not as she looked today. The Mrs. Stammerall in the photo was a young blonde woman with a bobbed haircut in a revealing short red flapper dress from the 1920s. She touched an aged finger to the picture and ran it along the contour line of the dress.

"That was my favorite dress," she whispered, more to herself than to Wilson and Hamish.

"It's a beautiful dress," Hamish said, peering over her shoulder.

"But how...?" She looked up at Wilson with bewildered eyes, but he too was staring intently at the picture, a dark glint in his eyes. "I don't understand, how is this possible? It's some trick; devilry."

"Isn't that you, Mrs. Stammerall?" Hamish frowned and looked at the picture with visible confusion. He pointed a slender finger at it. "See, there's the big red tent behind us and there's the striped one. Look, there's that man and the boy in the sailor suit that walked past us."

"Yes, but look how young I look; and that dress..."

"It is a very good picture, Mrs. Stammerall," Hamish agreed. "Don't you think so, Wilson?"

"Yes, an excellent picture." Wilson nodded.

"I don't understand, Mrs. Stammerall. Do you not like the picture?" Hamish gave the woman a confused look.

"Don't you see it? I am just a young girl in this picture." Mrs. Stammerall searched Hamish's face for an explanation, but he stared back at her with concern.

"You've been out in the sun all morning, Mrs. Stammerall. Maybe we need to get you home. Is your nephew still waiting for you in the parking lot?" Hamish

21

soothed as he gently placed a hand on her elbow and started to walk her towards the carnival exit.

"Yes, Jonah is waiting with the car. I think perhaps I need to go home and lay down for a bit." Mrs. Stammerall nodded as Hamish led her away.

Hamish escorted the older woman and spoke quietly to her as they walked away. He looked over his shoulder at Wilson and gave a barely perceptible nod, then they disappeared into the crowd of carnival goers. Wilson watched until Hamish's tall top hat was out of sight.

His stomach growled with a rumble of hunger, and he ran his boney hand over his belly, gazing up at the morning sun. It was early in the day, still many hours before he could eat.

CHAPTER 3

Wilson hung his head down as he sat in his booth. Unlike the other carnival workers he did not like to watch the crowds of people go by, trying to catch the eye of a passerby and lure them closer to make a sale as Hamish constantly instructed him to do. He watched the ebb and flow of the crowd from beneath the wide dark brim of his hat, a sea of passing legs and shoes, glancing up only when someone trod on the small patch of dry earth before his booth.

A black shape fluttered across his vision and landed a few feet in front of his booth. The large black crow tucked in its wings and slowly walked across Wilson's line of sight, its feet leaving a distinctive anisodactyl print in its wake: three toes facing forward and one, the hallux, facing backward. Wilson squinted and thought he could make out small talon marks in the dusty earth, one at the end of each toe.

The crow strutted back and forth in the small space before his booth— and Wilson genuinely believed that was what the bird was doing, strutting not walking. It even eschewed the thumb-sized end of a hotdog, which lay sprawled in the dirt beside the remnant of its bun, choosing instead to just strut in front of the booth, its head cocked slightly so its black eyes could stare constantly into the photo booth and at Wilson.

Wilson found the bird's presence infuriating, and he cast his eyes about the gritty bottom of the booth for a rock to throw at the creature. There was something about the bird's incessant pacing that gave him the impression he was the one in the cage and the crow was flaunting its freedom.

Fucking flying rat.

His camera, seated on the counter of the booth, cast an oddly triangular shadow across the ground, as if one of the Great Pyramids of Egypt had been toppled onto its side. Wilson glanced at the camera and then the crow, who had now stopped pacing and was watching him intently. He ran his tongue along the inside of his cheek as his gaze fell upon the lower lever.

What if I took a special picture of the crow? What would I see?

Wilson knew the camera saw people as they desired to be seen, as they saw themselves in their dreams and fantasies. Some dreamed of being younger or more desirable; others desired different lives altogether. The camera watched the movies in their minds and knew the roles they yearned to play. The camera saw it all and put it on film when he depressed the lower lever— the special lever.

Does a crow dream of being an eagle, or maybe a lion?

He fixed his gaze upon the crow and slowly reached for his camera, avoiding any sudden movements that would startle it into flight. Hamish would not be pleased if he used the camera so frivolously

But how would he know?

He stayed his hand for a moment, a deep frown crossing his thin lips.

Somehow Hamish always knew.

The crow suddenly took flight, quickly climbing skyward and away from Wilson's booth. He pursed his lips and watched until it was little more than a black stain against the threatening storm clouds.

All for the best I suppose.

He looked at the camera, a warm smile crossing his face; the kind of smile one reserved for a close friend or beloved relative. The camera had belonged to his uncle, Thomas, and the man had carried it with him on the long journey from England when he immigrated with Wilson's father to America in December of 1888. When he was a child, Wilson often heard his uncle speak of the brothers' long steamship journey from Southampton to New York. When the Titanic sank twenty-four years later, Thomas further embellished the tale with the detail that they had traveled the same route that sank the Millionaire's Special.

Wilson's father found work in a New York haberdashery selling hats while Thomas fell in with the underside of the city's criminal element, the Black Hand. His uncle was not a large or physically powerful man, but he proved a valuable resource to the criminal underworld with his camera; a camera that could produce a picture without the need for a developing room, a true thing of wonder in those days. This always struck Wilson as confounding. After all, what need did gangsters have of a photographer? However, that was before Wilson understood how special the camera was.

After the murder of Joseph Petrosino, the head of the police department's Italian Squad investigating the Black Hand, several police detectives sought personal vengeance against the organization and discreetly executed a number of known associates. Wilson's uncle was shot from behind by an unknown assailant while returning home from the German bakery one morning. The crime was never solved, but Wilson's father told well-wishers at Thomas' funeral that he was certain the police were the culprits.

Wilson was only nine when his uncle was murdered, and his father worked long hours to make up for the loss of the robust second income in the household. His mother was a cold and distant German woman, who scorned being the wife of a hat salesman almost as much as she did the pale, sickly child they raised. She thought life was grand when Thomas was alive and they had the financial resources to dine at some of the city's swankiest restaurants and drink at the most exclusive speakeasies, elbow to elbow with the gangsters she read about in the newspaper. After Thomas' death, she spent much of the day out of the house while her husband was at work, leaving Wilson alone. Then one day she never came home at all, ever again. His father just sighed and sat waiting on the couch that night, and then he never spoke of her again. He forbade Wilson to ever mention her name and that's how they moved on—as if she had never existed.

A small, shy, awkward child, Wilson often came home to an empty house, crying from the frequent abuse he received at the hands of his classmates. Several of the older Irish boys in the neighborhood took note of Wilson's English father and made it their personal mission in life to torment the boy.

One day, when he was thirteen, with tears in his eyes and his lip split and bleeding from the latest beating, Wilson ascended the stairs into the attic in search of the trunk full of his uncle's things. Thomas had been a gangster and Wilson thought perhaps there was a gun or truncheon among his possessions, something he could defend himself with against the local toughs.

To his disappointment the trunk contained no weapons, only old clothes and scuffed shoes. The ancient camera, his uncle's most treasured possession, lay at the bottom of the trunk, wrapped protectively in a woolen coat. The origin of the camera was a mystery to Wilson. His uncle once told him a story of a Canadian inventor who sent a prototype of his camera to England to work with a young chemist on developing a new kind of film. Unbeknownst to the inventor, the man was an occultist who believed that if the eyes were the windows to the soul, perhaps the lens could be the window to something even greater. The man conducted various experiments with the camera before gifting it to Thomas. The whole tale sounded preposterous to Wilson at the time, and he had discounted it as the whimsical musing of an uncle entertaining his young nephew.

Beneath the camera he found a photo album with pictures of women inside. Each woman had her own page labeled in his uncle's meticulously neat handwriting: Mary Anne, Annie, Elizabeth, Catherine, and Mary Jane. There were four pictures on each page; the first three pictures were taken in alleyways, drinking halls, shabby bedrooms, or on darkened streets. Wilson could see one blurry street sign, Hanbury Street, and thought maybe one day he would visit that place.

The pictures were shadowy with poor lighting and were sometimes grainy; the women were dressed in very revealing clothes or in some cases various state of undress. However, the fourth picture of each woman was brilliantly clear and, although the settings were the same, the women appeared quite differently. Two of the women wore fancy, expensive dresses, while another appeared to resemble a school teacher, and yet another the Queen of England. One even looked remarkably like a man, with short hair and a dark, bushy mustache.

Wilson found the pictures arousing. He briefly contemplated sneaking the album down to his bedroom but feared his father would discover it. That would mean a beating and then the album would be gone forever. Placing everything carefully back in the trunk to avoid alerting his father, he closed the lid and stroked the trunk.

I will come visit you girls again tomorrow.

That night, he lay in bed running his tongue over his swollen lip. Staring at the ceiling, he contemplated feigning illness to stay home the next day; a day without the taunts of his classmates; a day at home with his girls.

It was then that he heard the voice call to him from the darkness of his closet.

"Wilson."

The voice sounded friendly and far off but held an unmistakable hint of menace. It reminded Wilson of the neighborhood boys pretending to be a friend and calling him from across the street.

He stared into the closet, an impenetrable blackness

that seemed to swallow the light. Out in the hallway, a light shone as his father moved about the house. The narrow band of light that penetrated the room from beneath his door splayed across his room but vanished against the opaqueness of the open closest. An even greater blackness seemed to move within the darkness of the closet, a shape large and hulking.

"Wilson…" The voice was more insistent this time, more forceful.

Wilson's whole body shook with fright as he struggled to keep from vacating his bladder. His fingers dug deep into the sheets as his limbs went rigid with fear. Too frightened to move, for fear the thing would bolt from the closet, he moved only his eyes toward the door, mentally pleading for his father to come in, his throat too constricted with terror to call out.

"No, Wilson, no." The voice was rough and guttural but spoke to him in a soothing tone. "I am a friend."

"A friend?" Wilson's voice squeaked like a mouse.

"Yes, Wilson, a friend. I was your uncle's friend."

"My uncle?"

"Yes, Wilson, your uncle Thomas knew me well."

Wilson's body relaxed, if only slightly. He sat up in the bed, his back wet with sweat.

"Wilson, do you want to make those boys in school stop hurting you?"

Wilson nodded uncertainly.

How did this thing know about that?

"Good. Good. Do you want to get back at them?"

Wilson nodded again, this time more assuredly.

"Wilson, do you want to hurt them?"

"Yes." Wilson nodded, a tentative smile crossing his lips, "I do. I want to hurt them very badly."

CHAPTER 4

As the day wore on, storm clouds rolled in over the Midwestern plains and a light rain quickly gave way to a steady downpour, keeping away all but the most determined carnival customers. Wilson tucked his camera inside his jacket to keep it safe from the rain and stepped out of his booth.

The downpour ran off the rim of his top hat in small rivers as he sloshed through the muddy earth back towards his tent. As he walked, he noticed the other booths and tents closing up to shelter from the rain.

His route back to his tent always took him by the faded red tent that belonged to Bella. Wilson was not a sociable person and solitary by nature, but if he had a friend in the Grand Ole Traveling Carnival, it was surely Bella. She had joined the traveling carnival six months ago during one of their stops in Missouri; young and beautiful, Hamish was more than happy to find a place for her on the south side. Bella always talked kindly to him or smiled and waved if she saw him passing by.

Wilson felt heady and carefree whenever he was alone with her and one evening confided to her that the camera sometimes took special pictures, which was a violation of one of Hamish's rules. Sometimes he would tell her stories of how the camera saw people.

He told her that several years ago the mayor in one small Kansas town had threatened to shut the carnival down if Hamish did not make an exorbitant contribution to the man's campaign fund. Hamish had brought Wilson with him to the man's office in City Hall and had him take a special picture of the mayor. The camera saw the mayor dressed as a giant, man-sized baby with a great white cloth diaper. The judge was simultaneously embarrassed and furious at what he called a carnival 'parlor trick' and had them roughly escorted out of the building by several police officers.

Wilson had been terrified that the policemen would damage his camera, though he left out that part of the story when he told it to Bella. The way he told Bella the tale, he and Hamish strolled out of City Hall with the ringmaster clapping him on the back for a job well done. Bella laughed at the story, picturing the man as a big baby and imagining the look on his face when he had seen the picture. She laughed until tears rolled down her eyes; it was one of the happiest moments of Wilson's life.

Bella would always ask him what he thought the camera would see if he took her picture but Wilson would never do that. Wilson would never take a special picture of her. He would tell Bella he could not do that because Hamish kept close tabs on the inventory of the special film and she would pout.

Wilson liked when she pouted almost as much as when she smiled. He liked her pretty green eyes and her long auburn hair. She wore revealing dresses that would make

Wilson blush, when he glimpsed the fullness of her breasts or the outline of her nipples, though he never looked away and he was always careful not to let Bella catch him stealing those glances at her. Wilson liked the way she dressed. It reminded him of the women in his uncle's photo albums; but he knew this was her costume, just like the black suit was his.

Often Bella would read to Wilson as he sat cross-legged on the floor of her tent. The tent had a large square rug that made the space feel luxurious to Wilson and he would stare up at her transfixed as she sat upon her bed and read aloud. Sometimes, the stories were romances that bored Wilson, and he would just listen to the sound of her voice, reveling each time her green eyes glanced toward him and she smiled at the rapt attention he gave her.

Lately, she had read to him from a story called the *Strange Case of Doctor Jekyll and Mister Hyde,* about a doctor who attempts to find a serum to repress mankind's violent tendencies but instead creates a potion that transforms him into a murderous criminal. Wilson found his attention drifting during much of the story, as his place on the floor provided him ample glances up Bella's pale legs. However, he did find the part about Mister Hyde beating Sir Danvers Carew to death, until his cane broke upon the man's body, to be exhilarating and he looked forward to hearing more of the story and Mister Hyde's exploits.

When Bella's tent flap was closed, he knew she was in there with men. Wilson could hear them sometimes, grunting and panting, and that always made him angry. He knew he had no right to feel covetous of her. Bella had never looked at him the way he looked at her; Wilson was certain of that. However, the thought of another man touching her skin, making her make those noises, sometimes caused a well of anger in him to surge to the surface like a freshly drilled oil well. In those times, Wilson would find someone to take a special picture of and then things would feel better again.

Bella's tent flap was closed as he walked by but Wilson guessed that was likely due to the rain, like almost all other tents on the south side. That was ok; he did not feel like talking at the moment. He just wanted to get his camera out of the rain, and he wanted to feed. The sensation gnawed at him ceaselessly, rising from a dull pang to an insatiable craving.

The rain beat a steady rhythm against the canvas top of his tent as he slipped through the flap and secured it closed behind him, tying each of the cords that held it closed in tight knots. With great care, he placed the camera down on the wooden chest and hung his top hat on the coat rack before lighting the rusty lantern. The flickering light came to life as the kerosene-soaked wick caught fire, casting the room in a dancing light.

He quickly stripped off his wet clothes and hung them on the coat rack, leaving them dripping muddy puddles on the tent's dirt floor. He avoided looking at his reflection in the large oval mirror. The sight of his spindly limbs and boney ribs disgusted him, and he knew the wet strands of his hair would only accentuate the balding of his round head. Instead, he lay down on the bed and pulled the raggedy blanket over his thin, naked body, enjoying the protection it afforded against the chill air of the rainstorm. He noted with annoyance that the small hole in the tent's roof was dripping a steady stream of rainwater onto his bed, the droplets forming a maddening, rhythm tapping as they struck the bed, quickly dampening the blanket.

Tap. Tap. Tap.

Fucking flying rat.

He turned his head and stared at the camera, which seemed to stare back at him with its glass lens. Sighing, he wrapped his arms around his belly and curled his knees into a fetal position.

Across the room, the camera began to give off a humming sound, and a beam of bright light suddenly sprang forth from its lens, shining directly into Wilson's face. His eyes opened wide initially, welcoming the light, but then rolled back into his head as his body began to tingle. In the darkness of his mind, he felt a sensation of plummeting as if on a rollercoaster encased in total blackness. The first few times he had felt this, he had screamed in terror, but now Wilson embraced the feeling.

He took the ride.

***

Wilson was in total darkness when he opened his eyes, illuminated only by a small round window. Looking through it he saw his body curled up on the dirty bed, staring sightlessly toward the window. He turned away from it and held up his hands; thick, strong fingers tipped by sharp nails appeared before his face, and he clenched his fists, feeling the power in his grip. The sensation of his long, flowing hair brushing against his shoulders, as he looked down at his muscular body, thrilled him.

This is the real me.

"Yes, Wilson. Yes, it is. It's the way we were meant to be," the voice in his head, the voice from the closet, replied.

We.

They were two symbiotic parts of one whole. The voice in the closet could not take the pictures to open the pathways. It had no corporeal form in Wilson's world. Only Wilson could do that, and his uncle before him. In return, the voice shared its body and let him inside. However, Wilson was no mere passenger on this train; he was the conductor. He, Wilson, controlled the beast. His kills nourished them both. It took a toll on his physical body and sometimes he wondered if one day it would be reduced to a dried husk. Would that have been his uncle's fate had he not been murdered? In those moments, the voice assured him that they would share this strong, unstoppable body together forever.

Wilson knew he was in the in-between place now. He opened his mouth and let out a primal roar into the darkness as he waited, and an animalistic strength and power began to course through every fiber of his being.

This is how the lion must feel before it runs down the gazelle.

He embraced the darkness and ran the claw at the end of his thumb across its razor sharp twins on each of his fingers, making a loud clicking sound.

This is how God must have felt when he created the world.

"We are a god," the voice said, its tone dark and guttural.

The darkness reminded him of the emptiness that inhabited the closet of his childhood home at night, when the voice would talk to him and instruct him on the use of the camera. The camera did more than just see into their minds, to their secret wishes and heart's desires; it carved a pathway into their mind. Now Wilson just had to wait for that pathway to reveal itself.

There it was; a tiny pinprick of light in the distance. Wilson started to walk quickly towards the light. His gait quickened to a run, powerful legs taking long loping strides, propelling him towards it.

He felt the hunger building inside him as he rapidly approached the light, stopping just outside the perimeter to peer in. This was the threshold into Mrs. Stammerall's mind, a place where she was the star of the movie.

One thick-clawed foot at a time, Wilson entered the light and found himself in a moonlit alleyway lined with refuse and garbage cans. A light snow was falling. He looked up and saw the first flakes drifting down from the starless sky. He then glanced at a poster on the alley wall and stepped closer to look at it.

Stupid place for a poster.

Written in bright red letters across the top of the poster were the words 'A Merry Christmas.' Below that was a colorful drawing of Santa Claus with his arms around two smiling soldiers in the khaki uniforms and wide brimmed hats of doughboys from the Great War. The American flag was emblazoned behind them and in large letters the words 'Peace – Your gift to the nation' ran across the bottom of the poster.

Wilson sneered at the smiling faces of Santa and the two soldiers as he tore the poster down with one clawed hand. He crushed it in his hand and tossed it into the darkness of the alleyway as something skittered in the darkness, causing him to sniff its scent in the air.

"Rat," he growled in a deep, guttural voice.

Wilson's foot splashed through a cold puddle, dotted with snowflakes that quickly disappeared against the glassy surface of the water. He looked down at his reflection; long, rust-colored hair flowed down to his shoulders and framed a wide, brutish face with a flat nose and deep-set blue eyes looking out from beneath a heavy brow. The sight of his broad, powerful shoulders and muscled chest made the wide mouth, full of jagged teeth, open into an obscene grin.

This is the real me. This is who I was always meant to be.

His taloned hand rubbed at the pain in his side, the hunger now aching deep into his muscles.

"We're hungry, Wilson," the voice urged.

We need to feed.

The thought cut through the pain, twisting it and reforming it into desire.

"She's coming, Wilson. We want to hurt her. We want to taste her," the voice growled and Wilson nodded in agreement.

Wilson edged to the end of the alley and looked out. A man with dark hair, dressed in a black suit with white pinstripes and a matching vest and tie, walked down the street with a blonde woman in a red flapper dress—the dress from the photograph. They walked arm and arm with a slight stagger to their steps. Wilson sniffed the air and smelled the alcohol on them. He could hear the woman giggling as they talked in hushed tones. The man looked familiar to Wilson. If he recalled correctly, he was an actor from the old movies.

The thought made him snort derisively; the prudish

Mrs. Stammerall's fantasy of a night out in the arms of a Hollywood star was playing out before him. He imagined she dreamt of being wined and dined by the star and smiled at the thought that whatever else her dream held would not come to pass this night.

As the couple walked past the open alley, Wilson's clawed hand shot out and grabbed the young Mrs. Stammerall by the arm. She screamed in terror as he swung her hard into the alley wall with a sickening cracking of bone. The man in the pinstripe suit dissipated into the air as the tendril of imagination that dreamed him into being was severed.

The blonde woman lay crumpled on the alley floor sobbing, her left arm and leg bent at misshapen angles. Wilson's heart pumped wildly as he loomed over her before he grabbed her by the throat, lifting her off the ground. Mrs. Stammerall clutched at his arm with her unbroken hand, and her right leg kicked wildly against the wall, the left one just flopping like a dying fish.

Her blue eyes opened wide in terror as Wilson opened his mouth wide to reveal a maw of sharp teeth and breathed his hot breath into her face. She tried to scream but the pressure on her throat only allowed a squeaking noise to emerge.

Wilson did not care about this woman. He did not care about her hopes and dreams or the people that loved her and would mourn her. He felt her terror warm his body like sunshine against his skin and watched dispassionately as a tear rolled down her cheek and over the hand clutching her throat.

He breathed in her fear like a sweet aroma, the scent

exhilarating him. Wilson enjoyed this part most of all; the way their bodies trembled in trepidation, the feral sound of their screams, the look of anguish as he tore their flesh, and finally, the deep sadness in their eyes as he extinguished the light within them.

"Yes, Wilson, yes!" the voice in his head was exultant. "Break her!"

The hunger inside Wilson pulsed, and he sank his sharp teeth into her neck, enjoying the gush of warm blood that filled his mouth. Her blood tasted salty, and Wilson drank deeply as her slowing heart pumped the warm liquid into his mouth, his lips sealing around the open wounds until the blood had completely drained from her body. He continued to drink from the woman's limp form, supping ever deeper, draining her body of an essence and vitality beyond the physical. Some would call this the soul, but to Wilson it was a sweet nectar that satiated his hunger and sustained him. He gorged until all that was once Edith Stammerall was no more.

CHAPTER 5

Wilson awoke the following morning feeling full and content. Feeding upon Mrs. Stammerall would keep him nourished for weeks, but he felt a pang of regret at the thought that he would not feel the exhilaration of a kill again until the next town.

There were rules. No more than one per town. Not ever. But whose rule was that? Not his rule, certainly. Not the camera's rule, of that he was positive. It was Hamish's rule.

How he yearned to take a picture of Hamish. Sink his claws into the man's eyes and hear him scream. The thought made Wilson smile as he glanced at the camera seated on the wooden chest. He imagined pointing it at the ringmaster and seeing the fear in the man's eyes at the realization that it was Wilson, not him, that held true power.

One day.

He sat up and swung his feet onto the floor, curling his toes in the dusty Oklahoma dirt. Wilson glanced over at his pillow and frowned; a stringy clump of long, black, greasy hair lay deposited on his pillow as it always did when he fed. A memory of young Mrs. Stamerall suddenly flashed through his mind, causing Wilson to smile wickedly.

It was always worth a little hair.

He lifted his clenched right fist towards his face and slowly opened his hand. Two blood-speckled teeth lay in his palm alongside little pink indentations where the pointed roots had dug into his flesh as he clasped them tight. He did not fully understand how he could bring them back with him, but Wilson did not care. All he cared about was that he did; he always did.

Crawling over to the scuffed wooden chest, he slipped the metal key around his neck into the lock, clicking the mechanism open. He then placed the camera in his lap and lifted the wooden lid. The dark black cloth felt soft between his fingers as he lifted it away. Underneath were his treasures scattered over the bottom of the chest. A sea of white, dozens of teeth, stared back up at him as Wilson ran his hands reverently over them, his eyes gleaming with the rush of savory memories that assailed him.

He stared down at the teeth and felt his mouth salivating, a stirring feeling more akin to desire than hunger. Wilson did not always feed on them immediately like he had with Mrs. Stammerall; he often enjoyed playing with them and relished their final screams before sinking his teeth into their neck. Sometimes they broke and just whimpered as he fed.

He held the two new teeth between his right hand thumb and index finger and lifted them up to his eye to appraise them proudly. He leaned forward and ran his tongue over each of the teeth, feeling their every contour from the rounded top and smooth sides to the pointy bottom. They tasted of blood, and he closed his lips about them, sucking hard as he tasted the fear and sorrow that had become infused in the calcified tissue. Closing his eyes, Wilson smiled at the sweet memory the taste brought back to him.

He then carefully deposited the teeth along with the other tiny, white treasures he had gathered and placed the black fabric over them as if he was tucking them into bed for the night. He closed the lid and locked the chest, pulling the lock three times to ensure it was secure Then, satisfied that all was safe, he patted the trunk with his boney hand.

One day the trunk would be filled to the top with treasures.

***

Wilson sat in his booth, watching the steady pattern of raindrops like little bomblets cover the open field. The previous day's rain had continued unabated and kept away the summer crowds that would usually be packing the carnival at this time. He had not seen the carnival this empty on a summer's day since the Olympics in Berlin, a decade earlier, when that black man, Jesse Owens, had won four gold medals, causing the German chancellor to storm out of the stadium.

The sparse attendance would undoubtedly put Hamish in a foul mood. The handful of visitors, with their brightly colored umbrellas, stuck mainly to the north side of the carnival, moving from one big tent to another. Nobody would want a picture of their rain-sodden day at the carnival today.

Even during the war years, the crowds would come to forget their sorrows and fears for an afternoon. Those were good years. There was so much death in the world that no one noticed a few more.

He sat on his uncomfortable wooden stool, his hand supporting his chin as he leaned against the counter, daydreaming, replaying the night's events with a wicked smile. The more he daydreamed, the more he thought of the treasures in his wooden chest. Wilson felt as if the pearly, bloodstained treasures were calling to him. He wanted to return to his tent and run his tongue over them, lick them like a child with a delicious lollipop. Let the flesh of his tongue run over the rounded edges and pointy tips of the roots, tasting the blood. He would suck the teeth clean, every single one of them.

The thoughts began to build into a temptation he could not resist. Wilson glanced around, seeing Hamish nowhere.

Nobody will notice if I pop back to my tent for a few minutes.

At that moment, he spied the tall, lanky form of Long Li at one of the food booths across the way. The man wore a traditional black Chinese shirt and pants that Wilson always thought looked like pajamas. His shaved head was topped with a black skullcap, from which a long, thin braid of hair emerged and ran down the tall man's back. If Li spotted Wilson leaving his booth or saw it empty, he would surely spread the word.

"Meddling busybody," Wilson mumbled as he watched Li buy a spitted kebab of chicken meat from the booth.

He waited as Li paid and nodded his thanks to the man in the booth before heading back towards the meandering city of tents on the south side with his noonday meal. He pulled off large chunks of chicken as he walked, barely chewing the roasted meat before swallowing it. The man's long braid swung from side to side like a pendulum as he walked, oblivious to the rain.

To Wilson's chagrin, the rain lessened and stopped by the time he felt Long Li was safely ensconced among the tents and out of view. He sat there glumly as he spotted the first ray of sunshine poking through the thinning clouds. It would not be long before he would spot the first headlights of cars coming from town, making their way to the carnival and disgorging their eager occupants. His treasures would have to wait.

***

As darkness descended on the carnival that evening, the city of tents became a maelstrom of sparkling lights. The big tents on the north side looked like small mountain peaks illuminated against the darkness. The night was also the time of day when the south side came alive. With most of the respectable townsfolk home for the night, the town's more adventurous spirits would come seeking pleasures that the withered crones at the C.P.F.V.P.B. would find quite objectionable.

Wilson prodded the coin box underneath the counter with his foot, and it made an appreciable jingle. Hamish would be very happy with the day's take. Wilson decided to return to his tent.

As he tried to do each night, Wilson decided to walk by Bella's tent. He strolled past the myriad of tents, stopping to watch for a moment as a large bald man with a thick black mustache sat in his tent, tattooing a bright red heart on the forearm of a man seated with his back to Wilson. Several other tents had scantily clad women walking back and forth or smoking cigarettes on stools. They would often call him "cutie"—though Wilson knew he was not cute—and beckon him toward their tent or ask to take their picture, but he would instead keep his head down and walk past them.

As Wilson walked towards Bella's tent, he could see that her door flap was open, making him smile. He could sit and talk with her for a bit. Maybe she would read him more of the tale of Jekyll and Hyde. That would make him happy.

But Wilson's smile quickly faded as he spied the man in the black bowler hat. The rolled-up sleeves of the man's white shirt revealed tattooed forearms and a pair of suspenders that trailed up from his pants to run over broad, muscular shoulders—Karl, the barker for all the girls on the south side of the carnival.

Karl was talking to a man and pointing toward Bella's tent. He saw the man put several dollar bills in Karl's hand, and the barker quickly slid the bills into his pocket. He slapped the man on the shoulder before heading back into the crowd.

Wilson felt his anger rising as he watched the man walk towards Bella's tent.

The man was heavy-set and bald with a thick blonde mustache. He was wearing a grey epaulet shirt and dark slacks with a policeman's gold stripe down the side. Above the right breast pocket of the man's shirt was a small tin nameplate with the word "Hayes" etched in crisp letters and a deputy sheriff's shiny star adorning the space over his heart. A large pistol sat snuggly in a holster on the man's right hip, and a wicked looking black nightstick dangling from his left hip. The deputy sheriff looked into Bella's tent, but before he entered glanced from side to side to see if anyone was watching. He caught sight of Wilson, his eyes settling on the camera in his hand and narrowing in suspicion.

"Here now, what are you doing?" Deputy Hayes asked as he unhooked the nightstick from his belt.

Wilson looked down at his feet, not wanting to meet the man's eyes.

"Are you taking my picture?" The deputy walked over and poked Wilson hard in the chest with the round tip of the nightstick.

"I... I'm sorry, Sir," Wilson apologized but inside he felt a rage boiling. He hated getting poked, and he especially hated to be poked in the chest.

"Oh, don't mind him, Sir," Bella said, stepping out of her tent. "That's just Wilson."

Bella was wearing a short, black silky robe that revealed the bottom curve of her pale buttocks. Wilson had never seen so much of her backside before.

"I don't need people taking my picture." Hayes poked Wilson again in the chest with the nightstick so hard his top hat nearly tumbled off. "I was told this carnival was discreet. We have people in this town that would get ideas about me being here. Ideas I would not appreciate."

"Wilson meant no harm. He has a special camera. He's an important man here at the carnival," Bella said as she placed her hand on the police officer's shoulder.

"Special, how?" Hayes squinted his eyes at the camera. "It looks old as hell."

"It sees things," replied Wilson, holding up the camera. "Special things. I could take a special picture of you."

"What does that even mean?" The deputy's anger gave way to guarded curiosity.

Wilson grew up with men like this deputy sheriff; they had poked him and pushed him around his whole life. Men like this had killed his Uncle Thomas. He could see that the deputy was looking at him with thinly veiled disgust and he self-consciously tried to adjust his old, ill-fitting suit.

"Never mind, Wilson," cooed Bella. "Why don't we go into my tent for a bit?" she said as she sidled up alongside the deputy sheriff, stroking him across his chest.

"First, I want to know what's so special about this camera." Hayes eyed Wilson before turning his gaze to the revealing neckline of Bella's robe: "then we go in your tent."

Wilson did not like how the man looked at Bella and did not like his thoughts of the two of them in Bella's tent. He decided he wanted to take this man's picture very badly.

"Look, I'll show you." Wilson raised the camera and slid down the lower lever with a loud click.

The deputy sheriff tried to raise his hand to protest as the flash went off, forcing Wilson to step back to avoid having the man swat the camera away. The camera whirred as the picture slot spit out a palm-sized black photograph.

"I normally charge twenty-five cents for pictures..." began Wilson.

"I'm not pay you for a picture!" Hayes held the tip of his nightstick against Wilson's chest and snatched the photograph from his hand. "I never agreed to that."

Only the faint outline of the big man, his hand outstretched, could be seen. The picture slowly sharpened as Bella and the deputy sheriff looked down. Wilson saw that she had slipped an arm around the deputy sheriff with her face pressed against his shoulder, looking down at the picture. He could see the outline of her breast beneath the thin robe as it pressed against the man's arm and he felt a sneer cross his face. He did not wait for the picture to finish developing before turning to go.

"You can keep the picture as a present," Wilson grinned as his eyes blazed with malice. "I must be on my way."

Behind him, Wilson heard Bella let out an excited gasp. "See, I told you his camera was special!"

"But how?" Hayes stared at the photo in complete bewilderment.

The deputy sheriff gawked at the picture in his hand. It clearly captured the image of him with his hand outstretched. The surroundings were just as they were in real life, and so were all the features of his face, but the man's uniform had changed to the dark blue coat with the gold braided sleeves and bright golden star of his boss: the Sheriff.

CHAPTER 6

Wilson cradled the camera protectively as he quickly navigated his way back to the tent. A look of malicious delight filled his face. He seldom took special pictures of men, much preferring the camera's photos of women. Young or old, he did not care; he hungered for them all the same. He loved the way the camera saw them, just as it had captured the women in his uncle's photo book.

"Move!" Wilson hissed as he pushed through a throng of men and women.

He felt a pang of desperation and knew he needed to get back to his tent. Even now, the deputy sheriff was in Bella's tent. The thought of the man looking at her, touching her soft white skin, filled him with anger. He felt beads of anxious sweat run down his forehead.

Poke me in the chest.

He was seething with rage.

He pushed through the flap and into his tent, quickly tying it closed behind him. He then gently placed the camera on the wooden crate facing him and lay on his sweat-stained bed, not even bothering to take off his black suit and top hat. The mattress was wet from where the rainwater had dripped in unabated, but he did not care. He stared into the camera's lens and smiled wickedly as the beam of light sprang forth from the camera into his eyes. Wilson almost laughed as he felt his body tingle and his eyes begin to roll back in his head. He closed his eyes and let the darkness overtake him.

***

Sheriff Bo Hayes strode through the corridors of the police station as if a god among mortals. Blue-clad police officers snapped to attention as he passed.

He approached the frosted glass door that read 'Detective Bureau' and turned the knob. The brightly lit room smelled of coffee, cigarettes, and gun leather. A large picture of him, smiling as he shook hands with the governor, hung on the wall. Bo loved that picture and knew some day that would be him shaking hands with one of the state's sheriffs.

As he walked down the middle of the row of desks, his chest swelled with pride at how the detectives averted their eyes, unworthy to meet his gaze. Detective Tom Childs, the man who had beaten him out of the starting running back position on the high school football team, looked down at his desk, his brow covered in sweat at the thought of incurring the Sheriff's ire. A large-bellied policeman with the three stripes of a sergeant on his sleeve, and a fresh coffee in his hand, accidentally stepped into the Sheriff's path, and then, realizing his mistake, apologized profusely, nearly spilling the drink as he stepped sharply out of the way.

Sheriff Hayes remembered the sergeant's snide smile

and mocking face when the policeman had told him he had failed to pass the detectives exam. Now the man groveled for his approval like a redbone coonhound. Hayes extended his arm and shoved the sergeant further away with a dismissive glance.

The Sheriff's eyes fixed on the large-breasted blonde secretary with the very short skirt. She beamed at him as he walked towards her.

"Good morning, Sheriff!" Her eyes stared at him, adoring as a puppy waiting to be fed.

There was a time when Sallie Mae rejected him whenever he asked her to dinner. The unapproving way she had always looked at him made him feel small. But now, she was at his beck and call, happy to meet his needs—his every need.

"In my office now, Sallie Mae," He slapped her hard on the backside, eliciting a delighted squeal from the woman.

He strode into his office, adorned with numerous awards for bravery and heroism, and sat behind his large oaken desk. The Sheriff pushed his chair back from the desk, leaving enough room for Sallie Mae.

"Shut the door behind you, Sallie Mae," he ordered as the simpering secretary entered his office.

As she shut the door behind her, a large shape sprang forward, causing the image of Sallie Mae to dissipate into the air. The creature was large and muscular, with long, rust-colored hair and blue eyes that burned hot with malice. Hayes saw the creature's mouthful of jagged teeth as it moved impossibly fast across the room.

All Sheriff Hayes could do was get his hands up to

protect his face as the creature bounded over the desk, rapidly closing the space between them. The beast grabbed him by the wrists and jerked, the Sheriff's arms snapping like old, decayed branches. The sharp sound of cracking bone mixed with Hayes' screams of pain and terror.

Hayes stared helplessly at the creature as his broken arms hung uselessly at his sides. He watched in horror as the beast slowly extended one long finger, tipped with a sharp black talon, and held it before his face. It repeatedly poked Hayes hard in the chest with the outstretched finger, causing the Sheriff's chair to slide backward more with each blow. Once, twice, and then before the third blow, the creature reared its arm back before plunging it into his chest. The Sheriff screamed, his bladder and bowels emptying as the creature twisted the taloned finger. The flesh and muscle of the sheriff's chest shredded and the cartilage of his breastbone popped as the creature buried the finger deeper. Hayes' whole body shook so violently from the pain that the chair rattled loudly against the floor tiles.

With a sickening, sucking sound, the creature withdrew the gore-soaked digit from the Sheriff's chest and smeared it across the screaming man's face, leaving bloody streaks crisscrossing his cheeks. The beast grabbed Hayes and dug its fingers into the skin of the man's scalp and sunk its other clawed hand into his shoulder. The sound of the talons scraping his skull echoed in Hayes' head as the beast slowly peeled back the skin atop his head to reveal gory slick bone. Hayes screamed, crying uncontrollably as he beat futile fists against the creature's muscular chest.

The creature laughed, a wicked, malicious sound as it

bent Hayes' head back to expose the pulsing arteries of his neck.

Then Wilson began to feed.

***

Wilson awoke smiling. He sat up and brushed the greasy clump of dark hair from his pillow. A troubling thought momentarily crossed his mind: he had broken the rules. But then he shrugged it off. Why should Hamish tell him how to use *his* camera?

He added the man's teeth to his collection of treasures and then reluctantly covered them with the black fabric. A sudden uproar outside caught his attention, causing his eyes to look sidelong at the tent entrance. Wilson slammed down the lid of the chest and locked it. A cacophony of voices rose not far from his tent, far more commotion than was usual for the south side, even on carnival days.

He ran a hand over the wrinkles in his suit, trying to smooth them out and retrieved his top hat from where it had tumbled from his bed, brushing the dirt away before placing it on his head. He grabbed his camera, carefully cradling the precious device in his arm as he stepped out of his tent.

The bright Midwestern moon was high in the sky and the post-rain mugginess made him sweat instantly inside his suit. People were quickly walking past, gathering further down the row of tents. With a feeling of apprehension, he realized they were congregating over by Bella's tent.

Wilson tried to move through the press of people, arms wrapped around the camera to protect it from the jostling crowd. He grunted as a man elbowed him in the eye, nearly dislodging his top hat with the force of the blow as Wilson tried to move past. He glared at the man, a large freckle-faced farm hand in overalls, who gazed disinterestedly back at him.

Wilson saw Karl talking to a short deputy sheriff, feigning a look of naiveté at the officer's questions. Then he saw Bella. She looked distraught and Wilson noticed how her usually happy face was contorted into a look of horror. Tears streamed down her face as she held a thick blue blanket around her; two other carnival women from nearby tents had their arms around her consolingly.

Wilson pursed his lips as he stared at Bella. He bore no guilt at being the cause of her torment, albeit indirectly, or even sympathy for her anguish. All he felt was a growing irritation that it appeared increasingly unlikely she would be reading him any more of the Jekyll and Hyde story tonight. He wished all these people would just mind their own business and be on their way.

A murmur suddenly ran through the crowd, and he watched as Bella gasped and hid her face against one of the women's shoulders. Two carnival hands walked out of Bella's red tent with a stretcher held between them, a large form, covered by a coarse woolen blanket, lying sprawled across it.

The carnival hand in front stumbled on a stone before regaining his footing. Nevertheless, the awkward movement was enough to cause the woolen blanket to shift, revealing a bald head beneath. A cry went up from the gathered crowd as the Midwestern moon shone down brightly on Deputy Sheriff Hayes' face, pale and sunken, his mouth stretched impossibly wide, frozen into a rigor of terror. Blood trickled from his mouth, oozing from the gap where three of his bottom teeth had been removed. His eyes were so completely bloodshot there was not a speck of white remaining as the orbs stared lifelessly at the sky.

Wilson stared, transfixed by the sight, as others turned away in horror and the farm boy who had elbowed him moments earlier bent over and retched noisily. Several deputies barked angrily at the crowd, ordering them back away from the body, and Wilson slowly backed away into the shadows between the tents. Only when he was certain that no attention was directed his way did he slip away from the crowd. He was careful to walk slowly to avoid arousing any suspicion as he disappeared back into the safety of his tent.

***

Wilson lay in bed that night, untroubled by the night's events. The flickering light of his kerosene lantern illuminated the small tent as eyes drifted to his wooden chest, the camera sitting atop it. He had never seen what someone looked like after he visited them. The look on the Deputy Sheriff's face was vivid in his mind, and he kept wondering what all those women whose pictures he took looked like when people discovered their bodies. The thought excited him.

He smirked, thinking of the expressions on their faces when he had taken their pictures. The way they had looked down on him. How different they must have looked in the end. The terror, his terror, forever etched on their faces. They must have all had funerals with closed caskets. The thought made him chuckle.

He looked over at the camera and frowned. He always locked it away in the chest at night, but the thought of opening it with all the police officers around made him pause. What if some nosy cop stuck his head in the tent and saw his treasures? He could not have that; oh no, he could not.

A soft tapping at his tent flap caused his eyes to dart nervously towards the opening. Could this be one of them now?

Why would they need to speak to me? Could they have found the picture on the deputy's body? Did Bella tell them about the confrontation?

"Wilson?" called a soft female voice.

A woman at his tent? That was very unusual indeed. Wilson stood up and pulled on his black pants, cinching the belt tight around his waist. He thought about putting on his shirt but did not want to chance the woman leaving.

"Wilson? It's Bella. Are you awake?" called the voice.

He made his way to the tent flap and untied several of the knots to peer outside. Bella's tear-streaked face stared back at him, her eyes red-rimmed from crying. She still had the navy blue blanket wrapped around her, and a weak smile crossed her pale face when she saw him looking back at her.

"Wilson, can I come in?"

"Come in?" He chafed at the surprise in his voice.

"If I'm bothering you..." she started, but he quickly cut her off.

"Oh, it's no bother; please come in," replied Wilson, quickly untying the tent flap.

She smiled at him as she entered and Wilson felt a pang

of self-consciousness as he watched her take in the meager surroundings of his tent.

She said I was an important person at the carnival. What must she think now? There are no fancy rugs on my floor, no soft sheets on my bed.

"Is it ok if I sit down?"

"Yes, of course!" Wilson tried to hide the nervousness in his voice.

He felt a wave of horror at the dirtiness of his sweat-stained bed as she sat down on its edge. He hoped she would not think the wet spot on the bed from the leaky tent was urine. As far as he could remember, he had never had a visitor in his tent before. He crossed the tent and leaned up against the wooden chest. She smiled weakly at him, and he smiled back.

"I'm sorry for coming over so late, Wilson. It's just that I have had such a terrible day and I... I just wanted to be around a friend. You have always been so kind to me, Wilson."

He stared at her; her eyes looked so big and beautiful in the lantern light.

"Is it ok if I just sit here for a while, Wilson?"

"What? Oh yes, of course." Wilson picked up the camera and leaned against the wooden chest.

"May I have some water?" She pointed to the water pitcher and chipped glass on the little table. "I have been talking to policemen all night about what happened and I am just parched."

"Yes, please. Have all you like."

Bella took the glass of water and drained the contents. Wilson was pleased to see she did not feel the need to wipe the rim of the glass off before she drank, her lips touching were his had been. It was almost as if they had kissed.

She held the empty glass in her lap and stared down at it as her shoulders began shaking, and Wilson realized she was sobbing again. He felt awkward and did not know what to do, so he reached out one boney hand and put it on her shoulder reassuringly.

"Oh, Wilson, it was just horrible. That policeman just began to scream and scream. And then his face...." Bella's voice trailed off as her crying resumed.

Suddenly, the tent flap flew open with a loud snap, causing Wilson to jump up in surprise. Bella gasped as Karl angrily strode into the tent. Wilson could smell the pungent stench of whiskey from the man before he even spoke.

"What is this?" Karl snarled.

"Karl, please," Bella stood up from the bed, "I was just talking with Wilson."

Karl looked past Bella at Wilson's scrawny form, his boney hands clenching into fists. The carnival barker turned to look furiously at Bella, grabbing her roughly by the arm.

"You beg me for the night off because a man dies between your legs and you turn around and give it away for free?" A vein in his forehead pulsed as he yelled at her.

Bella began to sob, and Wilson's eyes darted nervously around the room like a trapped animal. In Karl's agitated state, he feared the man would lash out and smash the camera.

"Please, I was just talking," sobbed Bella, her shoulders shaking.

"If this wretch wants you, he pays like the others!" Karl pointed at Wilson. "There are no freebies."

Karl shook her arm roughly, causing her to cry out as his elbow struck the mirror's frame, causing it to rock back and forth.

"I... I have no money," Wilson barely got the words out before Karl brought one booted foot up to kick him hard in the gut.

The blow caused Wilson to fly backward into the chest, dislodging the camera from his hand. The air left his lungs in a sudden whoosh that caused a blackness to momentarily flash before his eyes. He frantically reached for the camera, trying to catch his breath as it tumbled. He snatched it from the air in the nick of time, his finger inadvertently depressing one of the levers and filling the room with a bright flash.

"No money, no whore!" snarled Karl. "Maybe the lion trainer will let you stick one of the goats before he feeds it to the lions for dinner."

Karl turned and pulled Bella out of the tent. Wilson caught sight of her sad eyes as she turned to look at him one last time before disappearing from his sight. The camera whirred and spat out a black square onto the floor.

Wilson quickly unlocked the wooden chest and safely stored the camera before further mishaps occurred. He sat sprawled on the floor, his back against the wooden chest, breathing hard. His ribs ached from the kick, and he ran his hands over what he was sure was a reddening boot print on his midsection.

He looked over at the mirror, relieved it had survived the encounter. The blow from Karl's elbow had swiveled it down slightly to reflect more of the floor. Wilson squinted at the reflection in the smooth glass and groaned. The mirror reflected the image of the picture the camera he had snapped when he caught it as it fell.

In the lantern's flickering light, the picture slowly developed to reveal a young girl clad in comfortable-looking pajamas adorned with strawberries. The girl was young, likely not even in her teens yet, but the face was undeniably Bella.

CHAPTER 7

Wilson lay in his bed, the picture crumpled in his fist. He felt the pull of the camera like a magnetic force and almost cried at his inability to resist it. The desire for the intoxicating rush he felt when he left this frail body behind was just too strong. The hunt. The kill. The treasures. They all awaited him; he just needed to look at the camera and take the ride.

Not Bella. Anyone but her.

He beat the mattress with one hand, teeth gritted in frustration.

Why couldn't it have been Karl? It should have been Karl. It was all his fault. He should be the one in the picture. Maybe I could make a trade: Karl for Bella?

He glanced sidelong at the camera, perched upon the trunk, then back up at the roof of the tent at the hole the bird had teased in the canvas.

No, that is not how it worked.

Once the camera took a special picture, the soul belonged to it.

To it or to me? Was there even a difference?

Atop the trunk, the camera whirred and hummed, but Wilson did not turn his head to look. It called to him; the pathway to Bella awaited him.

What if I just took another picture of someone else? Refused to go to Bella and just moved on?

The camera hummed again, almost angrily, and Wilson sighed. Even if he took a hundred pictures, he knew he would follow that pinhole of light and it would lead him to Bella. Maybe not the first or second time but one of them for sure. The camera took its picture; it demanded its soul.

What if I just smashed the thing?

He laughed mirthlessly because he knew he would never do that. Bella was his friend, likely the only friend he'd ever had, but he would never do that. He would never consign himself to a life in this frail body when the camera could make him a god. That was his true self, the Wilson he was meant to be.

To Wilson, Bella had seemed unlike any other woman in the world.

But was she really? Bella looked just like those other women in Uncle Thomas' pictures, and he found one after the other. Maybe I will find another Bella; maybe even a better Bella.

Besides, was Bella even really his friend? She never brought him soup when he was sick or gave him any sort of a gift. Did she go back in her tent and laugh with the deputy about the little man and his camera? He supposed that was possible, maybe even likely.

The more he thought about it the more he wondered if he even liked Bella at all. Did he enjoy her silly romance novels or her carnival gossip? No, not really. Yes, she was nice to him but maybe she just wanted a special picture.

Yes, that was very possible.

Wilson pursed his lips as he contemplated their friendship. Maybe he did not like Bella at all; maybe he only desired Bella.

If I desire her, I can have her.

Yes, that felt right to Wilson. The camera knew he desired her, and the camera had given her to him. How could he reject such a gift?

He closed his eyes and slowly turned his head to face the camera; it instantly whirred to life again, the shutter snapping open with a loud click.

The beam of light from the camera shone upon his eye; he could see the brightness through his closed lid. All he needed to do was open his eye and all that was Bella would be his.

Wilson opened his eyes.

***

Wilson stared through the window with distaste at the thin, crumpled form that lay curled on the bed, a purpling bruise upon his chest. He then glanced down at the powerful body be now the strength, the power.

If only I could stay like this always.

A brightness radiated behind him, and he turned toward the light. As if Wilson's limbs moved by instinct, his legs moved towards the light, accelerating. His heart pounded in his chest as he ran.

"You are a lion chasing down your prey, Wilson," the voice spoke in his head.

The hunger in his body filled him. The anticipation of the kill stirred something feral within him. He gnashed his sharpened teeth at the air as he moved closer towards the light.

He slowed as he came upon the glowing portal of light and stared into that sacred place in Bella's mind.

There she was, wearing white pajamas with red strawberries embroidered on them as she climbed into a large four posted bed clutching a cloth doll with bright ginger-colored yarn hair. The bed was laden with large, soft looking pillows and was covered by a pure white blanket with intricately woven flowers of various bright hues and shapes. Around her the room was filled with a myriad of dolls and stuffed animals. A wardrobe painted snow white sat at one end of the room beside a matching dresser topped by three Victorian-styled doll houses. The door to the wardrobe was slightly ajar, and Wilson could see it was packed full of colorful dresses. There was a vanity on the wall opposite Bella's bed with a large oval mirror mounted atop it, its frame decorated by carved wooden roses. A white teddy bear with coal black button eyes and a pink nose sat on a stool by the vanity facing Bella's bed; the bear leaned so far to one side it was a wonder it had not toppled to the floor.

Young Bella lay back on the bed, pulling the blanket up to her chin as her auburn hair splayed out on the plush white pillow. She tucked the doll in beside her, its ginger yarn hair mimicking her own on the pillow.

"Mother, Father, I am ready for bed!" she called, a broad smile of pure childlike joy on her face.

The door to the room opened and a tall mustached man

and a woman with the same long, auburn hair and green eyes that Bella possessed walked in, warm, welcoming smiles on faces beaming with adoration for the little girl.

"Hey now, Mr. Stuffings. You're falling over." The man crossed to where the white teddy bear sat and tried to seat it upright, but it slid back to its leaning position once he stepped away again.

"Father, you know his name is Mr. Stuffin!" Bella protested with mock annoyance.

Her father snapped his finger and grinned. "That's right, it's stuffing in the turkey and stuffin in the bear."

He joined the woman by the bedside and each bent over and kissed Bella on the forehead as she beamed up at them with delight.

"Good night, kiddo," her father said, patting her on the leg.

"We love you, dear." Bella's mother smiled lovingly down at her daughter..

Bella returned a smile that reached from ear to ear, "I love you too!"

Her father put his arm around his wife, and they walked to the door, looking back one last time at Bella with big smiles before turning out the light and closing it.

Wilson watched enthralled as the scene played out before him. Bella had never told him much about her life before the carnival, and for a moment, he wondered if what he was seeing was a desire to return to life in the past or a longing for a life that never was.

His mild curiosity at the scene faded quickly, burnt away by the primal desire to rend and tear, to taste blood and swallow down the child's soul. He felt his hands clenching and unclenching, the thought of having Bella in his wooden chest full of treasures making him smile wolfishly. He thought back on the Deputy Sheriff's gaping maw as the blanket slipped away from his corpse and revealed the three missing teeth. Wilson wondered if the teeth he brought back with him would be Bella's or the small teeth of the child.

She would be all his, and only his, evermore. No more men in her tent. He felt a brief pang of sadness that he would miss their talks and the way he felt when he saw her but it quickly passed.

Wilson lowered himself to lay flat on the floor then and slithered across the soft carpet like a snake. Once he was alongside her bed, he quietly rolled onto his back and slid underneath until his upper body was sticking out the other side. He felt the coal black eyes of the teddy bear on him and turned to look.

The bear listed heavily to the left, it's perfectly round black eyes appearing to glare balefully at him. Wilson frowned at the bear, disliking the uneasy feeling it gave him.

I will tear the stuffing from that thing when I am done.

Then he smiled and corrected himself.

Stuffin.

He caught sight of his reflection in the vanity mirror, the smile fiendish on his brutish face as he lay on the plush white carpet. He could see Bella in the mirror, laying with her head on her pillow, eyes not yet shut as she shifted about to find a comfortable sleeping position.

Wilson watched her as he raised one strong hand and sank his talons into the edge of the soft blanket; then, tugging it lightly, he waited.

No response. He glanced toward the mirror; the girl had stilled in the bed but had not moved.

Wilson tugged again.

Now he could hear the bed creaking as Bella moved atop it. Glancing in the mirror he watched as she quietly pushed back the sheets and leaned toward the edge of the bed, not yet daring to peak over the side.

He tugged again, harder than the last time and heard Bella gasp and the bed creak as she jumped back from the edge. He could hear the bed continue creaking as she moved about. Chancing a glance in the mirror, he could see she was now perpendicular to the edge of the bed and moving slowly towards it on her hands and knees.

He was surprised she had not called out for her parents.

Not that it would help.

Bella could simply glance in the mirror and see him lying there. He hoped she would not do that.

That would ruin the surprise.

The bed creaked again, and he stared up at the edge expectantly. A face appeared, small and round, encircled by long ginger strands of hair that hung down toward the floor. Round button eyes peered sightlessly down at him, and Wilson frowned as he stared up into the doll's face. He was tiring of this game.

The doll's face slowly receded from view as Bella slid it back, and then the bed creaked again as the little girl leaned forward.

Bella's familiar face, the face of his only friend, with her green eyes and auburn hair, peeked hesitantly over the edge of the bed. One hand clutched the little doll as the other gripped the edge of the bed, white knuckled with fear.

Wilson stared up at her.

"Boo!" He opened his eyes wide and bared his teeth menacingly.

Her face became transfixed in abject terror, and she screamed as Wilson pulled her from the bed, his mouth snapping closed as his teeth sank into her neck. Blood sprayed from the girl's neck, raining red droplets down upon the pure white carpet and sending a crimson streak slashing across the teddy's chest and face.

Wilson had told himself he would not make her suffer like the others, although now the voice inside his head raged for him to do so. Her body felt so small and birdlike in his grip. It broke so easily, giving up Bella's essence, her soul, with complete capitulation and nary a struggle or cry.

This disappointed Wilson immensely as the lithe, lifeless form of the girl slid from the bed. Her body made a squelching noise as it landed onto the blood-soaked carpet, pinning the little doll beneath her so that its round face peered over her shoulder, the fabric turning crimson with blood.

He slid out from beneath the bed and looked down at Bella. Licking the salty blood from his lips, the taste mixed with the sweetness of her essence which still lingered inside his mouth. There was no remorse for the little girl or the woman she was. He knelt down. Wilson would take his treasures back with him; then he would take his time and savor Bella forever.

CHAPTER 8

Wilson stayed in his tent the following morning until he heard the screams and knew they had discovered Bella's body. He had enjoyed Bella's fear and suffering, as he had with all the others, but had no desire now to see what he had wrought upon his one-time friend.

As he lay in bed, listening to the commotion taking place outside the tent, his eyes repeatedly drifted towards the trunk. He had taken more than his usual share of treasures from Bella but dared not risk opening the chest with so many policemen undoubtedly milling about the carnival.

He rubbed his thumb against the two smooth, round shapes in his hand; they were slick with sweat from his palm. He was not sure why he had decided to take the teddy bear's eyes with him after thoroughly eviscerating the toy, but he returned clutching teeth in one hand and the button eyes in the other. At least the buttons would not implicate him in any crime.

Three deaths in one week was going to arouse some consternation among the locals, even if Mrs. Stammerall's death was not linked to the carnival, which Wilson was certain would be unlikely since she had visited on the day of her death. He would not be surprised, however, if the C.P.F.V.P.B was not already outside, picketing in front of the carnival gate, demanding they move on.

Hamish would be livid with him, of that Wilson was certain. He had broken the rule, not once but twice; and both times with deaths inside the actual carnival, a violation of another of Hamish's rules.

No more than one death in a town and never inside the carnival.

He rubbed his hands against his temples, as he was beginning to get a headache. The narrow beam of light streaming in from the hole in the tent's roof flickered and Wilson squinted up at it. There was something up there, small and black.

He sat up and stared at the hole.

There is definitely something up there.

He stood on his bed, craning his neck to peer up through the hole at the dark shape.

It's that crow again.

He felt certain of it. The nuisance bird had returned, and he felt equally certain that all his issues with crows as of late boiled down to the same bird, though how such a thing was possible he did not know. How could the same crow be plaguing him in all of these cities? That seemed unlikely, yet Wilson could arrive at no other explanation.

He peered up at the dark shape outside the hole; whether in reality or a trick of his imagination, he felt the bird stare right back at him.

***

Wilson thought that a sufficient time had passed since the discovery of Bella's body to venture out to his photo booth. It had been several hours, at least. Besides, his bladder was painfully full, and he needed to get to one of the south side's outhouses or relieve himself in the corner of his tent. He had done that on desperate occasions before, but the stench became quite offensive even to his nose in the warm weather months.

However, just as he finished getting dressed and was preparing to leave, a new cacophony of shouts arose outside. Could there be another body? Wilson quickly dismissed the idea and pressed his ear to the tent flap. The shouting sounded angry, like an unruly mob. Had the C.P.F.V.P.B stormed the carnival? No, he did not hear any sounds of physical confrontation, only voices raised in anger.

Tucking the camera protectively in the crook of his arm, he untied the last of the tent straps and stepped into the bright daylight. He blinked several times as his eyes adjusted to the light, and he tried to orient himself toward the shouting. It was coming from the direction of the women's tents.

A man he recognized as one of the cooks from the chicken cart came running by his tent in the direction of the shouting. He was a broad-shouldered man with bushy black eyebrows and a thick mustache. The sleeves of his grease stained shirt were rolled up to reveal muscular forearms.

"What's going on?" Wilson called as the man passed.

"They are arresting, Karl," the man replied in a thick

Italian accent. "He killed that policeman and poor Bella. The fucker knocked out all her teeth!"

More than usual... but not all.

"Karl?" Wilson had to restrain himself from smiling until the man was out of sight.

This could not have worked out better.

He had to see this for himself, maybe take a picture, a real picture, to remember the day. Wilson felt positively giddy; all his problems were working themselves out. Even Hamish's ire might be soothed after this, although he was more dubious on that point.

A large crowd of carnival workers and onlookers had formed around Karl's tent. The shouting had largely died down, but the mood of the group was still angry as a ring of stony-faced deputies, nightsticks in hand, formed a semicircle around the entrance of the tent to keep the mob at bay. Wilson decided to hang back on the periphery of the crowd to steer clear of any trouble, his hand protectively around the camera.

As he stood on the outskirts of the onlookers, he overheard Long Li saying a Federal Bureau of Investigation man was looking into murders that seemed to follow the Grand Ole Traveling Carnival. Karl had done bad things to women, when he was stationed with the army in the Philippines after the war, and they suspected he was up to his old ways. One of the carnival hands said loudly that Karl was sure to get the electric chair and that made Wilson smile again.

"You press the button, we do the rest," a man standing next to him commented.

It took Wilson several moments to realize the man was talking to him. The man wore a gray fedora hat, a gray tie, and high waist pants of a slightly darker gray. He was clean shaven with a thin face and dark, intelligent eyes. The man's eyes were so dark they reminded him of the teddy bear's button eyes.

"Were you talking to me?" Wilson asked.

"Your camera." The man pointed at the camera in Wilson's hand. "You press the button, we do the rest. It's a Kodak right? That's their slogan."

"Oh." Wilson did not know what else to say. He tried turning back to watch Karl's tent but the man kept talking.

"I know a little something about cameras. You can say it's a bit of a hobby of mine. I have one of those new Polaroid Land Camera Model 95s at home. That's a Kodak Brownie, right?"

"I don't believe so." Wilson shook his head and tried to ignore the man.

"Yeah. Yeah, I am almost certain that's a Brownie." The man craned his neck for a better look. Wilson was about ready to tell the man to mind his own business, when he spotted the pistol holstered on his left hip.

A police detective.

The man followed Wilson's gaze and chuckled.

"Sorry, I should have introduced myself. Detective Tom Childs." The man smiled and extended his hand.

"Wilson," he replied as he shook the man's hand but did not meet the detective's gaze. The man's handshake was firm and his hands were cool and dry, making Wilson self-conscious about his own sweaty palms and underwhelming grip.

"Do something about that. It's like holding a dead fish," Hamish would chide him. "A handshake instills trust and confidence. Work on it."

Right now, Wilson felt like his handshake instilled anything but trust and confidence, something a trained detective would pick up on easily.

"So, can I see that camera?"

"I'd rather you not," Wilson replied, shaking his head.

"Oh? Why's that?" Childs took a toothpick out of his shirt pocket and popped it into the corner of his mouth, chewing on one end. Wilson looked curiously at the toothpick and Childs winked: "Trying to quit smoking."

"Oh," Wilson nodded, "it's just that taking pictures is my job. If you were to drop it…"

"You couldn't work," Childs finished his sentence. "I get it, pal. I feel the same way about my girl here."

Childs patted the handle of his revolver and then slipped his hand into his pocket. Wilson could not tell if the man was genuinely agreeing with him or making a veiled threat.

"How about this?" Childs proposed in a conciliatory tone. "You hold the camera out for me to see, and I'll just take a look. Sound good?"

"I guess that would be fine." Wilson gripped the camera in both hands, harder than he normally would to make a show of it for the detective that he was concerned for the camera's safety.

Childs stepped in front of Wilson, leaning down to

visually inspect the camera, then craned his neck to peer at the back of the camera.

"The old man was a bit of a camera buff. Got me one of these for Christmas when I was kid. It came in a green box with a Brownie on it. Remember those? That Canadian guy Cox drew them in books. No?" Childs stepped back and rubbed his chin as he looked at the camera. "Huh? Kodak stamped the leather on the back of their Brownies but yours doesn't have a stamp. What's that extra lever for? And that slot in the front?"

"It's an extra shutter lever." Wilson pointed to the lower lever, the special one, and hoped the detective did not ask for a demonstration.

"For double exposures?"

"That's right." Wilson lied but thought it sounded convincing.

"And the slot?"

"That's where the pictures come out," Wilson pointed to the slot in the front of the camera.

"Where the pictures come out?" Childs seemed genuinely surprised. "That camera has to be over forty years old!"

"Yes, it was my uncle's camera. He brought it back from Europe. I got it after he died so I don't know anything about it before that."

"After the war?"

Wilson shook his head. "No, before the first one."

"Well, your uncle could have been a rich man. I never heard of any camera self-developing film before the Land

Camera and that was just a few years ago." Childs tone remained friendly but his eyes looked suspicious to Wilson.

Wilson shrugged. "Like I said, my dad gave it to me when my uncle died."

There was a commotion by Karl's tent, and the crowd's ire returned as a group of policemen led the barker from the tent. Karl's hands were handcuffed behind his back, and his face looked bruised and swollen. He looked down as the crowd rained insults and catcalls down on him.

"Karl looks like he put up a fight," Wilson commented, happy to direct the topic away from his camera.

Childs slipped his hands into his pants pockets and glanced toward the officers leading Karl away. "Yeah, well, Bo was not the most well liked guy on the force but he was still police, and the boys don't take kindly to someone killing one of their own."

"And poor Bella," Wilson added.

"A lot of guys have had trouble since they came back from the war, but it takes a sick mind to kill a woman like that and then pull out all her teeth. Oklahoma's had the electric chair since 1915; if they find one of her teeth in his things, he'll be getting strapped into it for sure."

With Karl escorted away, the crowd began to disperse and Wilson was relieved to have a reason to extricate himself from the conversation with the detective.

"Have a good day, Detective Childs. I am sure everyone will be relieved to know they've captured the killer in our midst." Wilson turned to leave, but Childs placed a hand on his arm.

"One thing nags at me though. When we found Deputy

Hayes' body he was still in his uniform; well, his uniform was by his body," Childs commented, sliding his other hand out of his pocket. "But in this picture, he's wearing a different uniform. How do you explain that?"

It took all of Wilson's self-control to mask his mounting panic as he stared at the picture he had taken of Deputy Hayes now in Childs' outstretched hand.

"How do I explain what?" Wilson fixed his face into a look of confusion and glanced nervously up at the detective.

"I found this picture in the pocket of his uniform pants." Childs pointed down at the tent tops peeking out behind Hayes' outstretched hand in the picture, then to a pair of tent tops over by Bella's tent. "He must have been standing over there when this picture was taken."

Wilson made a show of inspecting the picture, then looking in the direction Childs had pointed. "I think you're right. That's over by Bella's tent where they found him."

"Yes, but this is not the uniform he was wearing in the picture." Childs tapped the image of Hayes. "This uniform is too dark."

"Well, sometimes when the film develops the shading can be off."

"True," Childs nodded then pointed at Hayes' arm, "but you see that braid? That's a sheriff's braid. It's not on a deputy sheriff's uniform. And the star is a sheriff's star, not a deputy's."

"Well, you said he was not wearing his uniform. Maybe he changed, like a costume. This is the south side of the carnival. Sometimes people like to wear costumes." Wilson felt sweat starting to run down his back and soak the collar of his shirt.

"Maybe." Childs pursed his lips thinking, then held the picture up towards Wilson. "Did you take this picture?"

"No, I don't think so." Wilson shook his head and tried to feign innocence.

"Really? You sure? Take a good look at it."

"I take a lot of pictures, Detective, but I think I would remember taking one like that." Wilson pointed at the photo.

"Hmm," Childs turned the picture around to look down at it. "You know we had a woman in town die just the other night. Her nephew said she was very upset about a picture she got at the carnival right before she died. I asked to see it, but he said it upset her so much that he threw it out. And wouldn't you know, the garbage men had already come and taken it away. Did you take a picture like that, Wilson? Of an old lady from town?"

"I don't rightly know. I have taken a lot of pictures since we set up here, but I don't remember anyone being upset with their picture." his heart was beating so loud he was afraid the detective could hear it.

"Here's the thing Wilson," the detective held the picture up and ran one finger along the edges, "I told you I was a bit of an amateur photographer, so I know Polaroid camera film produces a pictures that is three point one inches by three point one inches, a perfect square. This picture is a rectangle: three point two five inches by two point two five inches. That means the photographer used Kodak one-twenty film, just like the old Brownie cameras. But I have never seen a Brownie that could produce instant pictures.

Well, except for that one in your hands. How do you explain that?"

"I honestly don't know," Wilson shrugged. He thought he was doing a good job of looking outwardly calm, but inside HE wanted to run as far away from this man as he could.

"You know, neither do I." Childs slipped the picture back into his pocket. "It's a mystery, and I just don't like mysteries, Wilson."

"You're a detective. You solve mysteries. It's your job." Wilson offered a smile that did not quite reach his eyes.

"That's right, Wilson; and I intend to solve this one. I don't know what this picture has to do with Bo Hayes' murder, but there is a burr under my saddle telling me it does."

The detective stared stony-faced at Wilson, and he wondered if it was a technique he used to break suspects. Wilson thought he had seen something like that in a cinema show once.

"Wilson, if I ask around the carnival about you, what will people tell me?"

"That I take pictures," Wilson smiled, pointing toward his camera.

"Would they say anything else?"

"No, I don't think so." Wilson shook his head.

"Well, if you think of anything else, I would like you to call down to the police station and ask for me. Will you do that, Wilson?" Childs handed a business card to Wilson.

"Of course." Wilson nodded as he slipped the business

card into his jacket pocket. "Have a good day, Detective Childs."

"Have a good day, Wilson. I'll be seeing you around."

That last bit sounded like another threat to Wilson, but he was relieved to finally be free of the detective and quickly turned to head for his photo booth. As he turned away from Childs, the smile slipped from his face.

There, seated atop the tent before him, was the crow. The bird's head was cocked as if watching something of intense interest, and its coal black eyes were fixed directly upon Wilson.

CHAPTER 9

As soon as Childs was out of sight, Wilson crumpled the detective's business card into a ball and deposited it in a trash can, covered in sticky cotton candy and spilled sodas. The detective could talk to whoever he liked. Carnival people never talked to the police. At least never in a revealing way. The carnival would be moving on in a few days, and Detective Childs would become a thing of the past.

Besides, Wilson had far more significant problems than the police right now. He sat in his booth on the wooden stool, and although he stared down at his feet, he could feel Hamish's piercing gaze upon him. The carnival's proprietor stood in the booth window and tapped his index finger against the coarse wood. Unlike the mask of contorted anger Wilson expected to see, Hamish's face was unsettlingly calm—a prospect Wilson found significantly more troubling.

"This carnival is a very special place, Wilson, don't you agree?"

Wilson nodded, glancing into Hamish's face for only a moment before looking away.

"Do you know why this such a special place?"

Wilson again nodded.

"Tell me, Wilson. Why is this such a special place?"

"Because you find special people to be part of the carnival."

"That's right. I can just look at a person and realize there is something special and unique about them, and I find them a place in my carnival. Wilson, how long have you been with the carnival?"

"A long time."

"So you're not new here?"

"No, of course not." Wilson glanced up, genuinely confused by the question. He had spent his whole adult life with the carnival.

"And you understand that with so many special people here I need to make rules?"

Wilson nodded, his shoulders sagging.

"Wilson, do you understand your rules?"

Wilson looked up to try to explain, but Hamish held up a hand for silence, so he just hung his head low and nodded. His stomach hurt, churning and knotting with anxiety. He just wanted Hamish to be angry, yell, and get this over with. This line of questioning was so unsettling that his bowels were quickly turning to liquid.

"Did you know you were breaking the rules?" Hamish's voice was maddeningly calm.

Wilson hesitated and then nodded without looking up.

"And you broke them anyway?"

Wilson felt frozen with fear; he could not even bring himself to nod. Hamish only stared at him, so still he could not be sure the other man was even breathing. The ringmaster's piercing eyes felt like they were boring into his skull like a drill. Hamish said nothing further, and they sat there in silence for what felt like several interminable minutes.

"Do you remember where I found you, Wilson?" Hamish finally spoke as he gave Wilson a withering look.

"In Philadelphia."

"Yes, but where in Philadelphia?" Hamish raised his eyes upwards as if trying to remember.

"In the street." Wilson hunched his shoulders meekly.

"Oh yes, that's right. In the street. Do you remember what I told you?"

"You told me I was special." Wilson looked up at the carnival owner.

"And do you remember why I said you were special?" Hamish leaned into the booth's window so close that Wilson could feel the man's hot breath against his face.

"Because of my camera."

"Oh yes, because of your camera!" Hamish stood up and pounded a hand on the counter so hard Wilson jumped. "And what would have happened if I did not take you in?"

"Someone would have broken my camera." Wilson looked up at Hamish.

"Someone would have broken your camera."

Hamish reached into the booth, put his hand under Wilson's chin, and raised his head to face him. "And what would you be without your camera?"

"Nothing." Wilson's voice was quiet, almost child-like.

"You'd be nothing." Hamish's voice filled with menace. "We have rules, Wilson. You must follow the rules or you will be back on the street; and you understand what that means, yes?"

"Yes."

"Good." Hamish's face broke into a malicious smile. "You have yourself a good day then, Wilson."

Hamish straightened his red coat, tipped his hat back, and turned away from the booth as if nothing had happened. Wilson seethed with rage. He hated the carnival owner with a passion. He hated groveling before the man and following his rules. Who was Hamish anyway?

He watched the man striding away and felt himself fill with hatred. With a sneer, Wilson raised the camera and looked into the viewer; the image of the carnival owner with his red coat and pants and tall black top hat filled the viewport.

A grin of pure malice crossed Wilson's mouth as his finger slid onto the lower lever.

"I'll be seeing you soon, Hamish."

He pressed the lever downward—and nothing.

No flash.

No whir.

Nothing.

He pressed the lever again and still nothing.

Then Wilson suddenly realized Hamish had stopped

walking and was cocking his head as if listening to a tune only he could hear. The ringmaster stood rigidly still, and Wilson felt his blood run cold with terror. A wave of bile rose up from Wilson's stomach and he turned his head, vomiting a foul tasting mouthful of acidic spew onto the ground. It splattered on the ground in a gray-yellow star that only just missed his shoes.

Wilson wiped his hand across his mouth and clutched the camera to his lap. He looked out at the passing crowd, but the ringmaster was gone. Even his tall black hat was nowhere to be seen. However, over the din of the carnival crowd, Wilson was certain he could hear Hamish laughing.

CHAPTER 10

The hot sun had given way to evening, and the lights of the Grand Ole Traveling Carnival illuminated the night sky like a small city. Wilson watched the Ferris wheel lights slowly turning on the carnival's north end. The air carried the scent of popcorn, cotton candy, and roasted meats of questionable origin as he walked through the tents of the south side.

The din of the carnival's north side belied the popularity of the rides, shows, and spectacles, with townspeople looking for a distraction from their everyday lives. The dark attractions of the south side always gathered a more subdued crowd, but the heightened police attention brought on by the two deaths of the past week had kept away many of those that sought out the dark corners of the carnival.

Those that came to the south side tonight were mostly men either walking alone in the shadows, hoping not to be recognized by their neighbors, or more rowdy groups of teens looking for some of the thrills found on the south side..

Wilson ran his fingers lovingly over the leather skin

of the camera as he walked; the night air was cool and a pleasant respite from the sun of this dust bowl state. He walked past Bella's faded red tent. It was dark inside now, and he was sure the other carnival residents had already picked through her few positions and taken anything of value. Stopping, he stuck his head inside the tent's opening and breathed in deeply. The scent of Bella's perfume still lingered in the air, and the smell of it brought back a flood of memories.

He felt a stirring in his loins at the mental images of Bella's last moments. Adrenaline coursed through his veins as he recalled the feeling of his raw strength as he had overpowered and broke her. He swayed a little on his feet, lost in the moment, remembering her taste. The little man raised a thin hand to his neck and lightly touched his skin, recalling the panicked panting of her last breaths on his neck. The feeling made him groan quietly with pleasure.

"Excuse me," said a soft-spoken woman's voice, shaking Wilson out of his reverie.

He felt a momentary panic at his discovery as he turned around, but when he set eyes on the woman, his mouth opened in utter surprise. She was perhaps the most beautiful woman he had ever seen. Her skin was a porcelain white, and she had soft full lips and large doe-like dark eyes framed by jet-black hair, tied with a red ribbon that fluttered lightly in the cool night breeze. She wore a plain blue dress and held her hands nervously in front of her. The woman immediately reminded Wilson of sitting at the cinema and watching an animated movie, though the name evaded him.

"I'm sorry I did not mean to startle you." The woman wrung her petite hands nervously.

"Oh, it's no bother." Wilson gave her his most reassuring smile. "How may I help you?"

"I seem to have gotten all turned around out here; I cannot find my way back to the entrance. Would you be able to point me in the right direction?" Her voice had a sweet melodic tone.

Wilson felt a hunger for this beautiful woman unlike anything he had ever experienced. She seemed so sweet and young and innocent. His eyes lit up with thoughts of what he would do with her—to her. Her skin seemed so white and flawless that he felt himself salivating at the thought of her taste.

"I could do better than that." Wilson tried to hide the eagerness in his voice. "I can take you to the entrance if you like."

"I hate to put you through any trouble." She protested, though Wilson could see the relief in her eyes.

"It's no trouble at all."

She blushed. "You must think me a very silly girl."

"No, no. Not all."

This seemed to delight her greatly, and Wilson felt his face beaming with a wide genuine smile. He then gestured to his camera.

"I can even take a picture of you, free of charge!"

Hamish had warned him not to violate the rules again. One town, one feeding. But how could he allow this beautiful creature to slip away? She needed to be a part of his collection of treasures. He would deal with the ramifications later, even if Hamish kicked him out of the carnival. He wanted this woman in his collection.

"That is very kind of you, but it's too dark over here; the picture would come out dreadful." Her gaze cast about, looking at the shadows. "How about by the entrance? It was very bright over there."

"That would be wonderful!" Wilson felt exhilarated. "This camera takes very special pictures," He added, patting the lens lovingly.

"Wow!" Her eyes alighted with excitement. "I'm so happy I met you, Mister...."

"My name is Wilson," he said, extending his hand.

"My name is Dahlia." She shook his offered hand.

Wilson felt his heartbeat quicken at her touch. Her hand was soft and warm, and he could feel the gentle thrum of her pulse.

Wilson was usually a slow walker, but this evening he walked quickly, eager to make their way to the entrance. Dahlia did not seem to mind and kept stride with him easily. She explained to him that her grandmother had not wanted her to go to the carnival, but she had snuck out and come alone because she wanted to see the animals—the elephants most of all. They were her favorite.

A deep frown crossed her beautiful face as she told Wilson how sad she was to find the elephants were back in their corrals after finishing with their performances for the day, so she had decided to leave and lost her way. She wanted to get home before her grandmother realized she had gone out.

As she talked, Wilson felt himself staring at her. Dahlia was perhaps the most perfect creature he had ever seen. Her features were delicate and unblemished. Her simple blue dress hinted at what Wilson was sure was a perfectly formed body beneath. Her large dark eyes exuded a childlike innocence, and Wilson could barely contain his excitement at the thought of those eyes filling with pain and terror. He smiled to himself; he would take his time with little Dahlia.

"Here we are!" He grinned, pointing to the large white sign with red letters that read, 'Welcome to the Grand Ole Traveling Carnival' and underneath in smaller black letters, 'J. Hamish White, Proprietor.'

"Wilson, thank you so much!" Dahlia clapped her hands and bobbed with childlike delight.

"It was my pleasure!" Wilson raised the camera, "Now for that picture."

"Oh, Wilson, I hate to be a bother, but could you take my picture with the elephants?"

"The… elephants?" Wilson lowered the camera. "But they are away for the evening."

"I can come back tomorrow, in the morning. I will tell grandmother I went to get something to eat." Dahlia lowered her voice into a conspiratorial tone, "Oh, please Wilson, I would so love to see the elephants and get a picture with them. It would make me so happy."

Wilson was going to suggest he take two pictures, one tonight and one when she came back in the morning, but he saw how excitedly she smiled at him and felt his resolve weaken. He nodded, and she squealed with delight, clasping her hands together.

"Wilson, thank you, thank you, thank you!" Dahlia bobbed up and down.

"The carnival opens at ten, but if you can get here at nine I can get you in to see the elephants before their first show."

Dahlia's eyes opened wide in disbelief, "Wilson, really?"

"Oh, yes," he nodded, "but it has to be our secret. You can't tell a soul."

"I won't tell anyone, Wilson, I promise." Dahlia shook her head, and the beatific look on her face reminded him of a nun taking her holy vows.

"Ok then, I will wait for you right here by the front entrance," he said, pointing toward the front of the carnival.

"It's a date. Tomorrow at nine o'clock," Dahlia beamed. "I better get home, now"

"Ok," Wilson nodded his understanding.

Dahlia turned and hurried toward the exit. He watched her go, surprised when she turned to look back at him and wave exuberantly at him. Wilson raised his hand and gave her a little wave in return, eliciting a joyous smile on her face as she turned and hurried out the exit. He stood there watching until she had disappeared into the night.

He applauded himself for being very clever. Her grandmother did not know she had come to the carnival tonight. If the girl was going to sneak back to the carnival and not let anyone know, nothing would connect her death back to the carnival. They would pack up and be on their way in a few days. Hamish would probably never know he did it. Never know he broke the rules, again.

A feral smile crossed his lips. A wicked, malicious smile.

You are cleverer than them all, Wilson.

CHAPTER 11

Deke Reynolds leaned back against the locked gate of the carnival entrance and fished a cigarette out of the front pocket of his overalls. He looked at Wilson, his beady, deep-set, piggish eyes holding a glare of indifference as he lit the cigarette and stared at the smaller man. The man had the thick body and broad shoulders of someone accustomed to hard work and physical labor. His misshapen knuckles and crooked nose belied someone familiar with fighting, one of the qualities that made him a natural for dealing with anyone who tried to sneak into the carnival. It was a common trait in older boys of his age, becoming young men too late and missing the chance to fight the Nazis and Japanese during the war. They were eager to prove they were as tough as those veterans returning.

"Nine dollars." Deke exhaled a plume of cigarette smoke into Wilson's face.

"Nine dollars?" Wilson could not hide his surprise at the exorbitant cost. "A ticket only costs three to get into the carnival."

"Nine dollars." Deke tapped ash onto the ground. "Three

for me to unlock and open the gate, three to allow your friend to come in, and three to lock the gate up again so no one asks any questions."

Wilson was going to protest but then caught sight of a shock of jet black hair cresting the rise leading to the carnival site.

Dahlia.

He could see she was wearing the same blue dress as the night before, the red ribbon in her hair fluttering about her head as she walked.

Must be her best Sunday dress. She wants to look good for her picture.

Wilson reached into his pocket, producing a battered looking leather wallet and counted out nine dollars, which he then handed to Deke.

"Pleasure doing business with you, Wilson," Deke grinned, showing the wide gap between his front teeth as he slid the bills into his overalls.

"Just open the gate, please. She's almost here."

"Oh, yeah, where?"

Wilson curtly jerked his head toward the approaching young woman, and Deke turned to look in her direction. The carnival tough watched her approach with a leering gaze that Wilson did not care for.

Taking a long drag of his cigarette, Deke glanced sidelong at Wilson. "Change of plans, the price just went up to ten dollars."

"What?" Wilson stared at Deke's open palm as the man extended his hand toward him.

"A pretty apple pie like that," Deke nodded toward Dahlia, "any man willing to pay nine dollars, is sure as shit going to pay ten, or do I need to make it twelve?"

"Ok, ten dollars," Wilson fumed as he took the last remaining dollar from his wallet and handed it to Deke. "Now open it up."

"Ok, ok. Hold your horses," Deke shoved the dollar into one pocket and withdrew a key from another with his other hand.

He undid the lock and pulled the chain holding the gate closed free with a loud clatter of metal that made Wilson wince. He did not need to call any extra attention to the gate this early in the morning. The man swung the gate open just wide enough for a smiling Dahlia to step through, then he closed and noisily slid the chain back into place.

"Good morning, Sir," she greeted Deke as she passed him.

"Mornin'," he replied, then to Wilson's chagrin, gave her backside a leering stare as she passed. He would have thrown the man a sour look, but Dahlia did not seem to notice and Wilson did not want chance ruining the girl's buoyant mood.

"Wilson!" Dahlia's eyes were positively alight with excitement, "How exciting! I feel like you just smuggled me through the Berlin Wall!"

"Ah, but does Berlin have elephants?" Wilson extended his hand in the direction of a large pink and blue tent.

Dahlia grinned and gave an excited clap of her hands as she started walking alongside him.

"We're going to go in the back side of the tent.

That's where the elephants are before the show," Wilson explained.

"Oh, Wilson, I am so excited. Do you like movies?"

"I don't see very many movies," he admitted.

"Oh, I love the cinema. I practically grew up at the theater. I would sit watching all day and just get lost in the wonderful stories. You have to go Wilson, you just have too!"

"I'll have to try harder to find time." Wilson gave her a small smile.

"My favorite, my all-time favorite, was about a baby elephant in the circus. I watched the movie over and over again. Ever since then I have wanted to see a real live elephant." She gave a little hop and skip as she walked.

Wilson thought that sounded like a lot of movie watching and wondered how the girl could have had that much free time.

"Did your father work in a movie theater?" he asked.

"Oh, I never knew my parents; Grandmother raised me. For as far back as I can remember it was always just me and Grandmother, but she thought the movies were a waste of time. She said I was filling my head with nonsense. There was a drive-in movie theater just beyond the woods where I grew up. When Grandmother was away or sleeping, I would sneak out and hide among the trees and watch movies. She caught me once and was so mad. She said I was lucky it wasn't the police who found me out there spying on the drive-in. But I wasn't spying, I was *watching*, and the very next day I was out there again!"

Wilson glanced sidelong at Dahlia as she spoke. He

guessed she was in her early twenties but spoke with such a childlike wonder of things. A dark thought crossed his mind: what if she was a child in her fantasies just like Bella, her body breaking easily?

Dahlia's dark eyes were wide and filled with excitement as she prattled on about elephants and crickets; Wilson very much wanted to see that look extinguished by torrents of fear and pain as he gripped her, hurt her, and consumed the essence of her. She smelled faintly of flowers, an airy spring-like aroma that Wilson thought was very fitting for Dahlia, though he longed for it to be replaced by the acrid smell of her fear. He suspected that anyone so filled with the wonders of the world would cling desperately to life, prolonging her suffering and his pleasure. He felt the thought beginning to intoxicate him and forced his thoughts back to the here and now.

"Here we are," he announced as they reached the tent's rear entrance flap. The smell of animal manure wafted from the tent; the odor disgusted Wilson, but Dahlia did not even seem to notice.

Suddenly, the tent flap swung open and a dark-bearded man, barely over four feet tall with diminutive limbs, stepped outside. He was dressed in a baggy white jumpsuit adorned with three thick colored stripes: one red, one blue, and one yellow.

Dahlia gasped in surprise and held her hands to her chest as a broad smile spread across her face.

"What? You never seen a little person before?" the man snapped, his dark bushy eyebrows knitting in anger as he looked at her.

"No, I haven't," Dahlia responded in a breathless tone as

she stared at him in wonder. "Which dwarf are you?"

"What the fuck does that mean?" he snapped back.

"Dahlia," Wilson interjected, "this is Beorn. Beorn the Human Beach Ball. The elephants lift him up and toss him back and forth between them."

"Beorn doesn't sound like a dwarf name." Dahlia looked perplexed.

Beorn frowned at her, then turned his ire on Wilson, "What the fuck is wrong with this dimwit?"

"Hey, there's no reason to be rude. She's visiting the carnival, and you know Hamish doesn't appreciate when we're impolite to the locals," Wilson protested, hoping that invoking Hamish's name would quell the man's acidity before he spoiled Dahlia's mood.

"Well then, let her pay to see the show like everyone else," Beorn waved dismissively as he turned and stomped off.

"I bet they call him Frowny," Dahlia leaned over and said in a hushed tone.

The feel of her breath against his neck sent tendrils of excitement coursing through Wilson's body. She smiled conspiratorially at him and laughed, a sound that bordered on a giggle. He found himself smiling back at her; something about Dahlia's good humor just seemed infectious. He stared at her, mesmerized by how flawless she appeared. Dahlia's skin was smooth without any imperfection, her black hair appeared to not have a strand out of place even in the morning breeze, and even her nose was perfectly proportionate for her face.

Her apparent perfection made Wilson feel dirty and

ugly. He suddenly became very aware of the greasy wisps of hair that poked out from his beneath his top hat, the sallowness of his complexion, and the dark circles beneath his eyes. She probably lived in a nice home filled with beautiful things.

She was like a beautiful flower growing in a meadow, and Wilson was consumed with a desire to stomp on it until the stem was broken and every petal crushed into the dirt. His eyes fell upon her full red lips and lingered upon her perfectly white teeth as she smiled at him.

I will take them all. One at a time while you still live. You will feel every root tear free of your gums.

I will make you ugly before you die. I will ruin you.

You will weep for the monstrosity I twist you into. You will beg for me to end you; but I won't. Oh, no I won't.

I will make you suffer until I grow bored of your pain and then I will take the rest of you. And your treasures will sit in the cold dark of my trunk until I come play with you.

"Wilson. Hello, Wilson?" Dahlia was looking at him oddly. "Are you ok?"

Her voice snapped Wilson out of his reverie, and he realized he had been standing there gawking at her as he daydreamed. He cleared his throat awkwardly, stalling as he regained his composure and plastered a smile on his face. Seeing this, Dahlia's smile returned.

"Are you ready to see the elephants?"

"Oh, yes!" Dahlia bobbed up and down with excitement.

Wilson pulled back the tent flap and ushered her inside. The rear portion of the huge tent was portioned off from the customer seats and performing arena by a large red curtain that split in the middle to enable the elephants to pass from the holding corral to the performing area. Hamish had acquired the carnival's two large, gray female elephants from a private ranch in Texas, where their owner had saddled them with the atrocious names of Dina and Darla.

Dahlia squealed with delight at the sight of the two tremendous animals as they slowly milled about the wooden corral. They wore large, bright pink rectangular cloths on their backs with dangling tassels that swayed as they walked to and fro. Their massive heads were adorned with a brightly colored faux bejeweled headdress.

One of the elephants, Darla, scooped up some hay with her trunk and slid the yellowing green stalks into her mouth, to Dahlia's sheer enchantment, as they entered the tent. However, Wilson shared none of her joy as the tent flap closed behind them. He felt a cold streak of fear shoot down his spine for there, leaning against the corral watching the elephants was Hamish.

He's never back here.

Awash in dread, Wilson contemplated how he could possibly extricate Dahlia from the tent before Hamish spotted them, but she was already walking forward, eyes riveted on the two elephants.

To his horror, Hamish glanced over his shoulder at them and Wilson had a horrible feeling that the man had been waiting for them all along. He turned to face them, his showman's smile spreading across his face. A coyote grinning in the hen house.

"Wilson, so good to see you up and about so early!"

Hamish's eyes flashed golden-yellow as they moved to Dahlia, who seemed oblivious to his presence. "And who is this exquisite creature?"

"Uh, this is Dahlia," Wilson stammered.

Hamish turned to address her, but Dahlia's gaze was still transfixed on the elephants. He reached out and grabbed her hand, sweeping off his hat in a flamboyant gesture as he bent to kiss it.

Dahlia's enchantment seemed to shatter as he grabbed her hand. The smile disappeared from her face, replaced by a look of horror, and she pulled it back before he could plant his kiss. She took several steps back, looking aghast.

"I'm sorry, did I startle you...Dahlia, is it?" Hamish asked, his own face a mask of manufactured apology.

She only nodded in response, her dark eyes wide and doe-like. Wilson thought she looked like she might bolt from the tent at any moment.

"Dahlia, like the flower," Hamish said as he replaced his black top hat atop his head, a sly smiling crossing his lips. "But you're not a flower, are you, Dahlia?"

"No, of course not," Dahlia stammered as she stepped backward and slightly behind Wilson, placing him between her and Hamish.

"So strange, isn't it? I mean all names have meaning, yet we call ourselves by something we are not. I am not a Hamish, he is not a Wilson, and you are not a Dahlia. Names are almost like trickery. Though it would not be the first time I was accused of being a trickster." Hamish rubbed his chin as he waxed philosophically, then stared hard at Dahlia. "A wise, old woman once always told me what a tangled web we weave when we practice to deceive. Catchy, eh?"

Wilson heard Dahlia intake a sharp breath, and he thought he could smell fear on her.

"Your hat. Your coat. Are you the ringmaster here?" Dahlia asked as her eyes ran over Hamish's attire, as if really noticing for the first time, and Wilson thought he detected a slight tremble in her voice.

"Ringmaster and proprietor of the Grand Ole Traveling Carnival," Hamish grandly announced, accompanied by a slight bow.

"In that story about the elephants, the ringmaster was a bad man, a very bad man. I want to go, Wilson. I want to leave right now," Dahlia spoke quickly into Wilson's ear in a hushed tone that he was certain Hamish could hear perfectly.

"Forgive me, but I have a great deal to do before we open. I hope you enjoy your day at the carnival." Hamish tipped his hat then looked at Wilson. "Don't be gone from your photo booth for too long. I expect we are going to have a busy day."

"Yes, Hamish, of course," Wilson nodded as the ringmaster strode past him. Dahlia rotated to Wilson's other side, keeping distance between herself and Hamish as he passed.

"Wilson, I think I should go home now," Dahlia insisted as the tent flap closed behind Hamish. "Grandmother will be awake soon and notice I am out."

"Oh," Wilson made sure he sounded very disappointed as lifted the camera. "But you must get a picture with the elephants before you go."

She looked anxiously toward the tent flap, then back to the elephants, her smile returning as she nodded slightly. "I would love a picture with them."

"Just go stand over there by the railing," Wilson instructed, pointing toward the corral.

"Ok." Dahlia was beaming once again as she walked over to the corral, taking in the sight of the elephants.

"Just right there is perfect. Both elephants are even looking right at us," he said, stepping back and looking down into the viewport.

Wilson could see Dahlia through the viewing hole, standing perfectly framed between the two elephants, both now facing the camera. Her hands were on her hips, and she had a perfect smile. He depressed the bottom lever, and the flashbulb briefly illuminated them, making Dahlia giggle and blink rapidly. The camera whirred and the black photograph slid out from the camera. Dahlia eagerly crowded over to look and frowned deeply at the black square.

"It didn't come out," she pouted with genuine disappointment.

"Just give it a moment," Wilson reassured her. "The film has to develop, and when it does, you will be amazed!"

The two of them looked down at the developing film. Dahlia made excited little noises as her outline became visible, and the elephants became clearer with every passing moment. As her image became more visible, she became even more excited, but Wilson began to frown. He felt his mouth turning down, and his brows furrowing, as the picture became fully developed.

He stared at the picture; Dahlia looked exactly like she did standing in the forefront with Dina and Darla in the background. There was absolutely nothing different about the photo than real life.

Did I depress the wrong lever? I could have sworn I pressed the lower one.

"You don't like it?" she frowned, seeing the disappointed look on his face.

"It's just that I think I could do better," Wilson muttered, trying to cover up his confusion.

"I don't know, Wilson. It's getting late, and I need to get home. I think the picture looks just grand."

"Just let me take one more," Wilson said, slipping the photo into his jacket pocket.

"Well, ok. Just one more and then I have to go." Dahlia smiled and nodded.

Dahlia took up the same pose, though Dina and Darla were now facing each other. Wilson held the camera steady and looked to make sure his finger was on the lower lever. Then, looking down into the viewport, he took another picture. The camera whirred and produced a black square. Wilson and Dahlia stared down as the picture developed. The outline of the two elephants, the corral, and Dahlia became visible, and just like before, she looked precisely the same.

"Oh, Wilson, you were right; I like this one even better." Dahlia plucked the picture from his hand and pressed it against her heart. "I love it, Wilson. Thank you."

Wilson stared from the picture to Dahlia and back

again. Something like this had never happened before.

Was the camera broken?

He felt queasy at the thought. If the camera was broken, could he fix it? He did not have the slightest clue how to do that. What would happen to him if it was?

Even worse, did that mean he would not be able to visit Dahlia tonight? He did not think that was the case; after all, the camera took the picture.

He was lost in thought as they walked back to the carnival gate, which was now open for the day. Dahlia appeared oblivious to his preoccupation, chatting incessantly and staring at the picture as she constantly pointed out new details she noticed.

"Look how their tassels appear to be moving."

"Oh, look how short their tails are!"

"One...two...three...four...they have five toes!"

"Their ears are much smaller than I thought they would be; in the story they were so big."

"See, they don't have tusks, Dina and Darla must be from Asia instead of Africa."

Finally, she just sighed and clutched the picture to her chest again as they approached the gate. "I cannot believe I saw real, live elephants."

Wilson smiled weakly at her, still lost in his thoughts.

"I am so happy I met you, Wilson." She beamed as she patted him on the shoulder. "I hope to see you again one day. Take care!"

He watched as she turned and walked quickly out of the carnival, turning one last time to wave at him before disappearing into the crowd of oncoming people. He stood there dumbfounded for a moment, perplexed at what had happened. Then, sliding the first picture from his pocket, he looked down at Dahlia's beautiful face smiling up at him.

A wicked smile slowly crossed Wilson's lips as a deep malicious hunger burned away the last of his perplexing thoughts.

"Oh, you will see me again, Dahlia," he sneered, a wide, lascivious grin splitting his sallow face.

CHAPTER 12

Wilson lay naked atop the cot's stained sheet, the night air cool upon his pale skin. The flickering light from the tent's lantern reflected off the camera's lens as it sat dormant on the wooden chest. He glanced over at the camera and then at the picture of Dahlia in his hand, staring at her fine features. He gazed longingly into her large dark eyes, picturing how they would look when he came to her that night. The surprise. The terror. The pain.

Wilson frowned at the picture, troubled that it seemed to capture her exactly as she was. He looked back over at the camera. No light. No whirring. It sat dark and silent on the trunk.

Was it broken? Had whatever magic that gave it its power run out?

No, that did not seem right. It still functioned the way it always did.

Was it Dahlia then?

Wilson knew the camera captured how people desired to be. Was it possible that Dahlia was so perfect that she was exactly how she had wanted to be? He could understand how other women could want to look like Dahlia; she was perfection. But did Dahlia really not desire more than to live the life she lived?

He studied the picture and was utterly amazed that there was absolutely no difference. She did not desire to be taller or shorter, for her hair to be longer, or even her breasts to be larger.

Wilson could feel his eagerness to see his prey again, his hunger to feed upon her soul and rend her life from the fabric of the world.

He smiled to himself, enjoying the building anticipation. He replayed the day's events, savoring his memory of her every movement. The sound of her laugh. The feel of her hand. He licked his lips as he recalled every feature of her face.

I took two pictures of her. Two special pictures. The camera should be hungry. Why is it waiting so long?

As if it heard his thoughts, the camera whirred to life.

It is not broken!

Wilson's anxiety and anticipation rapidly transformed into intense desire. A thrilling sensation coursed through his body, soaking his mouth with saliva and curling his toes.

Eagerly, he turned to face the camera, opening his eyes wide in acceptance as the beam of light sprang forth from the circular lens and struck his eye with the electrical charge of a bolt of lightning. He moaned with the ecstasy of the connection, a wolfish grin crossing his face as his hands clenched and unclenched in anticipation.

Wilson's eyes rolled back in his head, looking like two

egg-like orbs bulging from his sunken eye sockets, and felt the blackness begin to overtake him. He welcomed the roller coaster sensation, knowing that he would soon be gorging himself on Dahlia's terror and pain, and heard a wicked laugh leave his lips as the blackness took him.

***

The crow's eyes flew open, his heart beating very quickly as he came instantly to full wakefulness. He never liked to fly at night; there were other things that hunted at night, in the darkness, things he did not wish to contend with. However, he felt propelled by an unseen compulsion. He was needed.

The cool night air met him as he soared high above the carnival, now dark and slumbering below him. He banked, diving quickly to land upon the roof of the gray tent.

Without thought or reason, driven only by the undeniable need to do so, the crow began to pull at the opening in the roof. No longer simply plucking at strands, it was now ripping and tearing the canvas. His sharp beak cut like a knife, slashing at the hole with a singleness of purpose.

***

When Wilson opened his eyes again, he delighted at the feel of raw strength flowing through his limbs. He smiled when he looked at his strong hands with their black-tipped talons, hands made to rend and tear. His shoulder muscles bunched as he turned his head towards the light, enjoying the feel of his long, rust-colored hair brushing along his naked back.

The pinprick of light that pointed his way into Dahlia's mind already awaited him. He started for the light at a run.

In his mouth, his tongue flicked over sharp, jagged teeth, teeth that would soon bite and taste Dahlia's sweet flesh. He salivated at the thought, a long string of drool slipping down his chin, savoring the rush of power pulsing in his veins.

The light drew closer, growing like a sun in the darkness until it filled his vision. He stopped just outside the perimeter of the glow and ran his rough hand over the outer edge. Just one more step and he would be inside Dahlia's mind, within the place where she held her deepest secrets and desires. The violation of such a sacred, personal place aroused him nearly to the point of pain.

He peered into the light; it was a bedroom with a plush pink blanketed bed. It had four large posts, just like Bella's, with a lace canopy that hung like a silken spiderweb over a bed adorned with soft, round pillows. Wilson stepped into the light. The bedroom had a thick carpet that felt softer than grass beneath his clawed toes. He smirked at the movie posters adorning the walls: animated princesses and fairy tales. There would be no Prince Charming for Dahlia. The sightless eyes of a myriad of finely dressed dolls filled the other wall of the room and watched as Wilson stalked into the light.

I will make her watch as I break all her pretty things.

He bore an intense hatred for the girl that sprang from a dark well deep inside him. She had done nothing to him except show kindness. Regardless, he felt an intense, insatiable urge to mar and defile her, to reduce her to a quivering ruin of a person stripped of all hope and happiness. Wilson wanted Dahlia to know only pain and despair before he consumed her soul. He would lick the tears from her face, taste her sorrow. Revel in it. Her perfection incensed and offended him in a way he did not fully comprehend.

The feeling was more intense when he was in this body. It always was. He could feel a presence in his mind when he was in this body, watching through his eyes, feasting upon the pain he inflicted and feeding on the souls he took. He knew it was the voice in the closet. He was a monster with two brains.

"You are not a monster, you are a god," the voice from the closet spoke inside his head.

Yes, I am a god.

Wilson nodded in agreement.

Something dangled above Dahlia's bed, and he leaned closer to look. A small palm-sized hoop hung down above her pillows; there was a fine white cord in the center that traversed the circle, touching the hoop in eight points with a solitary dark bird feather hanging down from the bottom.

A dreamcatcher.

Wilson plucked the feather from the hoop and crushed it in his immense palm, enjoying the satisfying pop of the feather snapping in half. He flicked the dreamcatcher with his finger, propelling it to swing violently back and forth above the bed.

It didn't catch me!

He noticed an open door on the far wall and could smell the fresh scent of the outdoors blowing through. He stepped into the doorway and beheld the panoramic scene of a wooded glade. Tall mountains rose in the distance beneath a sun-filled cloudless sky. A gentle breeze blew across a green grass field and wildflowers stretched from the door into the wooded glade. He could see where footsteps, Dahlia's footsteps, had crushed down the soft grass. He smiled, causing a fresh strand of saliva to drip down his chin. Wiping his mouth with the hairy back of his hand, he began to follow her trail.

Wilson followed the trail into a forest of tall oaks and pines, branches and pine needles crushing under his mighty feet. He heard rushing water and could see a hint of blue ahead. His heart began to beat faster, a heady euphoric feeling that intoxicated him as he felt the end of his hunt nearing. Soon the fun would commence.

The trees changed from oaks and pines to white-trunked aspen trees, their fallen branches leaving scars on the tall trunks that resembled so many eyes. He could hear Dahlia humming over the rushing din of the river, the sweet innocence of the sound feeding his animalistic hunger.

At last, he came upon her, still dressed in her blue dress with the red ribbon in her black hair. She was humming a tune from a children's movie he did not know by name. Wilson recalled that one of the women who worked the south side had changed the lyrics to "Wilson is a jerk" and would hum it whenever he was passing by.

Dahlia leaned forward, her outstretched hand running nimble fingers through the river's water. Wilson saw his shadow fall over the young girl and noticed with delight that her humming had stopped and she had frozen in place. He panted, expecting what would come next: she would turn and see him, her terror would spread, she would scream.... He licked his rough lips.

Dahlia turned her soft white face to Wilson, and to his

great dismay, she smiled.

"Wilson!" her eyes danced with excitement. "I knew we would see each other again!"

He felt the wolfish grin slip from his face in confusion, and for the first time, shock of apprehension sliced through his muscular body. He stepped closer to the river and looked down at his reflection. He half expected to see his scrawny form looking back at him but was relieved it was his reflection's brutish face, muscular chest and shoulders, piercing blue eyes, and long rust-colored hair.

"See, Wilson, I have a mirror, too," Dahlia cooed, smiling as she brushed her hand over the water's surface and the river stopped. The water turned as placid as glass.

Wilson's reflection stared back at him from the calm water and then began to change. The reflection changed to an image of himself as a thin, dark-haired teen sitting on the floor of his bedroom back in New York. He was looking at a photograph of men sitting on the stoop of a small house talking together as a baseball, bat, and small pile of baseball gloves lay piled on the cement walkway of the home. One of the men, a policeman, appeared to be telling a story and the other two, a fireman and a man dressed in the khaki uniform of a soldier, were frozen in time as they laughed uproariously. None of the men were looking at the camera, giving the shot a candid feel as if they were unaware it was being taken.

"Those Dolan boys were very cruel to you, Wilson. Look at them, Jimmy wanted to be a policeman and Tommy a soldier. Angus wanted to be a fireman just like their father. I told Grandmother that it was their fault that they never got to grow up. They made you do what you did."

An uneasy feeling filled Wilson, spreading from the back of his mind through his body. The feeling came from that other presence within him. He had never sensed such a sensation from it before and it disquieted him.

"But Grandmother sees everything. She sees every tendril of the weave. She watches for bad children."

Wilson stared at the water, transfixed, as the image changed to his father sitting on the green couch in their living room, drinking heavily from a glass filled with dark liquid, a nearly empty bottle of whiskey by his feet.

"When word spread around the neighborhood about the condition their bodies were discovered in, your father knew, Wilson. He knew you went into the attic and discovered your uncle's camera. Your father hated himself for not destroying that camera. He was too weak and afraid of what would happen if he tried. He blamed himself for what you did. He couldn't let the horrors begin again. He had killed his own brother outside that bakery to make it stop."

The image shifted back to his bedroom.

The dimly lit room was suddenly bathed in light as the door flung open and his father staggered inside. Wilson watched as the teen turned around in alarm, cowering against the bed as his father pulled open the drawers to the small writing desk and then the dresser, upending each as he searched for something. The contents of his desk scattered across the floor, littered among the clothes tossed from his dresser— his pen, papers, books... even the woodworking kit he had received for Christmas the year his mother left them.

"Leave this place, Wilson," the voice in his head, the

voice from the closet, commanded him.

But Wilson could not leave or even move. He stared at the scene unfolding in the reflection of the water. He remembered that night so well. His father had reeked of alcohol as he ranted, his words slurred by rage, whiskey, and tears as he screamed at Wilson for going where he was not allowed to go and touching things he was never supposed to touch. He rounded on Wilson, demanding the boy give him the camera. His father was so upset with him. He had grabbed him and pulled him to his feet; the man's face was bright red and contorted in anger as he yelled, their faces so close that the alcoholic stench on his breath had stung Wilson's eyes. He demanded to know where Wilson had hidden the camera, poking him in the chest to accentuate each word as he screamed at him.

Wilson remembered the terror in his heart when his father's head turned to look at the closet, a feral snarl on the man's face as he released him. In the water's reflection, he could see the boy stagger backwards, free of the grip on his shirt. His father dashed towards the closet door, the combination of drink and debris on the floor making him slip and fall to his knees, but he crawled frantically forward and pulled open the half-closed closet. The boy took several tentative steps forward, wanting to shout at his father to stop.

Wilson's father crawled forward into the closet, the upper half of his body hidden from view in the reflection. The man violently tossed shoes behind him as he dug in the closet searching for the camera. The boy was terrified; Wilson still felt the fear even now, knowing his father would discover the camera secreted in the back corner of the closet at any moment.

As he stood on the riverbed, Wilson's eyes found the hammer from his woodworking set deposited among his scattered belongings on the floor; in the image, he saw the boy look at the hammer as well.

"Wilson, Leeeave," the voice in his head ordered.

Wilson watched as the boy in the image bent and picked up the hammer and walked toward the closet to stand behind his father, who was still on his hands and knees rooting about in the closet like a winter boar hunting truffles. The boy raised the hammer and brought it down, out of sight in the closet. His father's legs jolted, his body slackening and flattening against the floor. The boy lifted the hammer and brought it down again and again so mechanically that it reminded Wilson of a cuckoo clock his mother had brought from Germany. The clock had had a wooden carving of a man cutting a log with a saw and a second man with an axe who would bring the axe down on the mechanism's bell on the hour, one chime for each hour.

He watched as the boy brought the hammer down on his father. Five o'clock. Six o'clock. Seven o'clock.

The boy stood, staring into the closet as his father's legs twitched violently and then went still. The hammer, dripping with blood, bone, and gore, slipped from the boy's hand and clattered onto the floor beside his father. He then bent over, reached into the closet, and withdrew the small leather box—the camera. Then, as calmly as if preparing for school, the boy walked to his bed and set the camera down. He stripped off his bloody clothes and donned a clean shirt and trousers from the clothes scattered about the room. Retrieving a backpack from beside the bed, the boy dumped out the school supplies and stuffed the backpack with clothing. Then, without a second glance at the unmoving body of his father, the boy slipped on the backpack, picked up the camera, and walked out of the room.

Dahlia moved her hand and the image faded, again replaced by the rushing river. She looked at Wilson with large dark doe-like eyes that seemed filled with sadness.

"You were not a good boy, Wilson. Grandmother told me you were not a good boy."

Wilson felt rooted to the ground, a tremble rippling through his mighty limbs. Dahlia reached her hand into the pocket of her dress and withdrew the photograph he had taken of her. She looked down at the picture and smiled.

"I love the picture you took of me, Wilson," she beamed as she looked down at the picture. "I look so pretty in it."

Then, her face clouded with darkness, and she looked back at Whim. The voice in Wilson's head made a sound like a whimper.

"Grandmother said you only like me the way I want to be. But you would not like me the way I really am. Is that true, Wilson?"

As he stared at her, the dark pupils of her eyes began to grow until they consumed the whites of her eyes.

"Is that true, Wilson?" Her voice became hoarser.

She stood up, and Wilson watched in horror as her arms lengthened until the skin split and thick, black, hairy limbs tore through it. He took an involuntary step backwards as the beautiful features of her face began to lose shape and the skin of her face began to split, mandibles and a gaping maw beginning to tear through her perfect features to reveal a large mouth with rows of wicked-looking teeth. Two more long, black, hairy legs burst forth from Dahlia's chest and another pair tore through her back.

The voice in Wilson's head screamed, a primal sound filled with dread and terror.

The creature's mouth opened, the voice now shrill and painful to his ears. "Am I still beautiful, Wilson?!"

Wilson watched the creature shake off the last of Dahlia's skin and stand erect on eight long legs that protruded from an immense, round, black, hairy body. Eight shinning obsidian eyes stared darkly at him from atop a mouth full of jagged fangs.

The giant spider moved towards Wilson, and he turned and began to run. Fear filled the beast as it ran through the forest, the sounds of Dahlia scurrying after him close behind. The scars on the aspen trees seemed to blink like so many thousand eyes watching him.

"I would sit in the trees watching the movies, Wilson. I watched all the movies over and over again. I loved the princesses the most," he heard Dahlia saying in a hoarse-sounding roar. Wilson felt a scream leave his lips, the feral scream of prey fleeing its hunter.

He ran across the green field, trampling the wildflowers under his taloned feet. His heart beat not with excitement now but with terror for the first time. He felt fear inhabit every fiber of his body and pushed his powerful legs to take him through the door and into Dahlia's bedroom.

He caught sight of the movie posters again, and with growing horror, realized his mistake. The camera had seen Dahlia exactly how she desired to be. The creature that pursued him now had dreamed in the deepest reaches of its heart to be like a movie princess and that is precisely what the camera had seen. He had failed to see through her façade.

Wilson ran out of the light of the room and into the darkness. Before him, he could see the light coming through the window into his tent, and he ran towards it with desperation. A mewing noise was coming from his mouth, and he felt the cold sting of tears streaming down his cheeks. He could hear Dahlia close behind him, but she too was now in the darkness, and he could not see her.

"Run. Run. Run. Run," the voice in his head repeated, its own intense terror mingling with Wilson's.

The light streaming in from the camera's lens was growing closer. Wilson just needed a few seconds more and he would be back in his tent. He just needed to place his hand on the window, and he would return to his body on the other side of the lens. He felt sheer terror inhabiting his very being and knew his only chance was to hurl himself through the window onto the other side.

"Willllsoooonn," Dahlia's voice called, rising in pitch until the last syllable reached an ear piercing sharpness.

The sound reverberated through the darkness.

The voice in his head screamed a mindless sound of pure terror.

Before him, Wilson watched in horror as cracks formed across the window. They began as small cracks in the center and then spider webbed across as Dahlia's high note pierced the darkness. He could hear the window cracking and then a deafening boom as it blew outward into his tent.

Noooooo.

The shattered window was so close now, the jagged edges of the round frame looking like a mouth full of razor sharp teeth. Wilson pushed off with strong trunk-like legs and leaped for the window. He could see his sweat-stained bed with his scrawny naked form writhing on it, mouth moving in a soundless scream. The powerful muscles of his body rippled as he dove for the window.

He fell just short, his flailing arms striking the frame. His fingers grasped for purchase, and he screamed in pain as the jagged glass cut through the thick skin of his fingers. He could feel the ragged tips of the glass scraping against the bones in his hands. He desperately tried to pull himself up and through the window as the muscles in his arms and back strained to lift his bulk through the opening.

A strangled cry escaped his lips as the thin strands of a silken web tangled around his legs, binding them tightly together. By the flickering light from his tent, shining through the destroyed window, he could see long, thin strands of silk stretching into the darkness. Somewhere behind him, he knew the strands ended with the gaping maw of the hideous spider. The thing that was Dahlia pulled on the strings until his body was horizontal in the darkness.

He squeezed his hands down hard upon the window frame, the glass cutting deeper into his flesh. He pulled with all his might, and his body began to slowly move toward the open window.

I am stronger than her.

A laugh escaped his lips. He would escape the creature yet.

Help me!

It was not a plea, it was a command, but the voice in his head did not respond. He felt it cowering in the dark corner of his mind.

Wilson roared in defiance and pulled himself closer to the window. He felt Dahlia desperately trying to pull him back, but he was stronger. One more pull and he could get his arms through the window, then the rest of his body. He would use the serrated glass to sever the silken thread.

A shadow passed in front of the window.

Someone is in my tent.

The shadow loomed closer to the window, as if peering inside. The bird's black head looked massive in the window. Wilson's eyes opened wide in horror as the crow's beak descended, pecking at his fingers. The whole of the crow's head filled the window as the sharp tip of its beak struck repeatedly, tearing skin and shattering bone.

Screams of pain escaped Wilson's lips as the crow's unabated attack mangled his hands, loosening his grip. Behind him, Dahlia gave a fierce tug that further destroyed his grip upon the window. He could hear the sound of ripping flesh as his hands tore free of the window, and he swung back through the darkness.

He hung suspended in the dark as he frantically kicked and swung his legs, trying to break free as his body pendulumed through the impenetrable blackness. The window was now a distant pinprick of light, far from his reach. The voice in his head groaned miserably.

More silken threads shot from the darkness, tangling in his long hair, and he felt a reverberation ripple through the tendrils of the rapidly forming web. The thoughts in his head were frantic as he looked up and saw the spider's large, bloated black body inching its way down a silken strand. Wilson felt the hot flush of urine run down his legs as terror emptied his bladder.

As the spider edged closer, he redoubled his frantic efforts to free himself. Then, he froze as a bright light exploded beside him, as if someone had thrown open the curtains in a darkened room.

On one side of him was blackness, an emptiness devoid of substance, but on the other side was a sprawling sandstone-walled canyon bathed in bright sunlight. Warm, dry air rushed in from the canyon like an exhalation of breath, and Wilson felt as if he could fall out of the darkness and tumble down the steep walls of the rock face before him. Along the cliff walls, he could make out small, square adobe dwellings, though he saw no people. Further along the wall, he spotted ancient petroglyphs depicting animal figures, spirals, snakes, and most prominently, carvings of spiders.

Dark specks lined the canyon rim, and a murder of crows sat quietly roosting beneath its cool lip. They sat in hushed silence; like a crowd awaiting the ringmaster's entrance into the big tent. Was he the show?

His eyes were drawn to the canyon's southern rim, where two monolithic sandstone spires intertwined and towered eight hundred feet above the canyon floor. The stone of the spires were a sepia color, but where the sun touched the stone it blazed a brilliant red-orange. Wilson could see that one spire was slightly higher than the other and both were topped with a layer of rock as white as bone.

Something moved near the top of the tallest spire, and he squinted to make out the shape. It moved along the edges of the sepia and white stone.

"Oh no," Wilson groaned, shaking his head as he

watched two long, black legs crest the top of the spire.

As it came to stand upon the spire, Wilson could see the spider was immense, dwarfing Dahlia by easily tenfold. The creature's eyes were a depth of black so utterly complete they appeared to consume the sunlight above rather than reflect it. He had seen eyes like that before, on the bear in Bella's room. He realized now why the eyes had perturbed him so immensely; it was this creature watching him.

"It's She Who Climbs the Spires, the weaver of the world, the purifier. Wilson, you fool. You have undone us," the voice wailed, absent of all strength and power, filled now only with fear and despair.

"Before Grandmother the universe existed in a state of chaos. There was only the dark, what you call the in-between place, until she weaved life and color into the world. She made everything in nature connected, like one living body. But when one part becomes sick, the whole body is affected. You are a sickness, Wilson. The creature you have become pollutes the body and defiles the world Grandmother has created," Dahlia explained.

The voice inside Wilson's head uttered a pitiful moan.

Dahlia's voice called to the creature from above him. "Look, Grandmother, look what I have brought you."

Wilson's eyes stared into the darkness, sensing Dahlia's presence more than seeing her. Returning his gaze to the giant spider atop the spire, he watched it bend its legs and spring forward in a leap that carried it across the sky like a black sun. He watched as the massive form sailed across the clear azure blue sky of the canyon, crossing the threshold from light to darkness and disappearing in the blackness above him. Despite its massive size, the creature landed with such finesse that it barely registered a tremble along the silken cords binding him.

Inside his mind, the voice shrieked in terror, a long mindless scream that did not end.

Wilson glanced upward and released his own scream as he felt the giant spider's hot exhalation wash down over him.

**

Wilson's body hung enshrouded in a silken cocoon up to the nose. His eyes were wide with terror and tears flowed unbidden down his cheeks. He moved his mouth beneath the silken shroud in an unintelligible whimper. The stench of his vacated bowels and bladder assailed his nose.

There was something moving above him.

As his gaze trailed upwards, he thought he spied eight eyes glaring back at him in the darkness, and the silk covering his mouth barely contained his blood-curdling scream. He bobbed momentarily on the silken chords and then jerked upwards. The sounds of his terrified shrieking filling the impenetrable darkness.

He came to a sudden stop in the darkness. Sobbing in terror, his powerful body immobilized, Wilson felt his blood run cold.

"Willlssssoooon," came Dahlia's voice out of the darkness, "Grandmother gave you to me. She is very cross with you, Wilson. You have been a very bad boy."

He leaned his head and saw eight dark, shiny orbs staring back at him, seeming to glow in the darkness.

"Wilson, you could have chosen kindness, but you came here to hurt me. You reveled in the thought of my pain and suffering; you and that other thing inside you. Wilson, I am going to eat your eyes and suck all the meat from your bones," Dahlia's voice was hoarse and vaguely feminine. "I am going to drink your soul. I am going to devour both of you. It's going to hurt, Wilson. It's going to hurt oh so very much, and I am going to make it last a very... long... time."

CHAPTER 13

Long Li's curved knife slashed down through the opening of Wilson's tent, slicing easily through the ties that had secured it. Daylight flooded the tent as Li pulled the flap back wide enough for Hamish to enter without removing his top hat.

The ringmaster covered his nose and mouth with a handkerchief as he entered the little tent. The stench was overpowering, and the carnival owner wrinkled his nose in disgust. He glanced up at the hole torn in the roof. Shreds of canvas hung down like a broken spider web, but the opening did little to vent the foul odor of the space.

Hamish gazed around Wilson's tent at his few paltry possessions until his golden coyote eyes found the camera. He walked over and looked down at the ancient camera; its shattered lens was broken into tiny slivers of glass that glinted in the light of the flickering lantern.

"Pity." He frowned at the ruined camera.

He turned to look dispassionately at Wilson, his limbs curled in upon themselves. His neck was stretched upwards, and his mouth froze open in a silent scream. Wilson's eyes remained rolled back in his head, and the skin around the bottom of his eyes drooped downward, the rims red and raw. He had bitten off his tongue, and the chunk of flesh lay covered in flies on his pillow. Hamish could see maggots wriggling in the cavities of Wilson's nose.

The man had fouled his bed in death, adding to the putrid smell. There was a large splatter of bird waste splattered across naked chest, a final ignominy in death.

"Is he dead, boss?" called Long Li from outside the tent.

"Oh, he's quite dead," Hamish nodded without a touch of emotion in his voice.

"I'll tell the boys to start digging a hole," called back Long Li.

"Here now, what's this?" Hamish's eyebrows rose in surprise.

He reached over to the little table and grabbed the glass of water, unceremoniously pouring out its contents. Leaning over Wilson's body, rigid with rigor mortis, Hamish scooped the glass against Wilson's taut neck.

"What have we here?" Hamish held the chipped glass up to the lantern's light.

Inside the glass, a small black spider peered back at Hamish, and a broad smile crossed the carnival owner's face.

"I know you. I knew you from the first time I saw you in the elephant tent. You were afraid I would tell your secret to Wilson, but I didn't." Hamish tapped a finger on the glass. "You see, I know your grandmother, too. She Who Climbs the Spires and I go back a very long way, to before there were stars in the sky."

The eight black eyes of the spider stared back at Hamish.

He looked down at the camera, then back to the spider. "The camera is just a broken antique now; there's nothing special about it anymore. I suspect when you killed Wilson and that thing, you destroyed whatever... well, whatever made the camera special."

"That means you're probably stuck here. The carnival is heading West into New Mexico, then Arizona. There's a place I know there, the Canyon de Chelly, where we can get you home. Until then, Dahlia, stay with us. You can watch the elephants all day. Does that sound good?"

Three loud clicks followed by a loud caw filled the tent, and Hamish looked up to see a large black crow staring down through the hole in the roof.

A warm smile crossed Hamish's face as he pointed up toward the crow and turned back to the little spider. "See, your grandmother's friend will be right here watching over you."

He tilted the open mouth of the glass onto his shoulder, and as if in acceptance of his offer, the small, black spider scurried across the red fabric and tucked itself protectively under the jacket's black collar.

Hamish smiled as he turned and strode out into the daylight, and the fresh morning air, without giving Wilson's body another glance. Long Li stood outside waiting for the ringmaster.

"The boys are digging a hole," Li said without any emotion.

"Good. Bury the body. There's no need to leave any

marker," Hamish instructed the man, "Use the key around his neck to open the trunk. I want you to take care of this personally, Li. Smash what you find inside with a hammer. Use the blacksmith's anvil so they're pulverized into dust, then brush it into the fire."

"Will do, boss." Li dipped his head in acknowledgment.

Hamish looked up at the bright, clear sky and smiled. It was going to be a good day, a busy day.

"Dahlia, a man once told me that life is a circus ring, with some moments more spectacular than others," Hamish addressed the spider as he walked. "And young lady, what you will see here will truly be spectacular!"

ABOUT THE AUTHOR

Jack Finn

Jack Finn is a horror author and active Horror Writers Association member living in the wilds of the Pacific Northwest with his wife and two fiendishly clever dogs. He is a lifelong believer that the Tooth Fairy proves you can trade body parts for cold, hard cash.

His books include, The Wolves of Kalinin werewolf duology: Prey Upon the Lambs (Anuci Press 2025) and The Desolation of Hunters (Anuci Press 2025); the horror collection They Come When You Sleep (Velox Books 2025), a re-envisioning of the Dracula mythos in the standalone novel The Seven Deaths of Prince Vlad (Crow Street Press 2023), the folk horror collection, Legend of the Deer Woman (Crow Street Press, 2023), and the forthcoming Book of Alice duology (Edge Weaver Books, 2026) and It Pierces (Crows Street Press, 2026).

His short stories have been included in Terrorcore Publishing's DOORS OF DARKNESS, January Ember Press' HORROSCOPE 4, Dark Village Publications' TWELVE MONTHS OF HORROR, Voices From the Mausoleum's HOWLIN' FOR YOU, Edge Weaver Books TALES FROM THE CURSED EDGE, and the upcoming WITH TEETH anthology supporting the Lakota Wolf Preserve.

SOCIAL MEDIA

INSTAGRAM:
https://www.instagram.com/therealjackfinn/

BLUESKY:
https://bsky.app/profile/therealjackfinn.bsky.social

TWITTER:
http://www.twitter.com/therealjackfinn

THREADS:
https://www.threads.com/@therealjackfinn

FACEBOOK:
https://www.facebook.com/TheRealJackFinn

TIKTOK:
http://www.tiktok.com/@therealjackfinn

WEBSITE:
www.therealjackfinn.com

BOOKS BY THIS AUTHOR

Red Queen, Yellow King

Wonderland has fallen. And something older than kings has taken its place.

A dark re-imagining of Alice in Wonderland and Peter Pan against the nightmare landscape of the King in Yellow's Carcosa.

It Pierces

A folk horror tale for fans of The Ritual and The Only Good Indians

Culling Of The House Of Boars

Perfect for fans of Empire of the Vampire, The Passage, and Game of Thrones.

Culling of the House of Boars is a descent into darkness where ancient vampire clans wage brutal wars among themselves, their hunger for power rivaling their thirst for human blood.

Prey Upon The Lambs (Book 1 Of The Wolves

Of Kalinin Duology)

In the tradition of Brotherhood of the Wolf, comes a terrifying werewolf tale in the final days of Czarist Russia.

The Desolation Of Hunters (Book 2 Of The Wolves Of Kalinin Duology)

As whispers of the wolf spread across the Russian Empire, Obrechen becomes the hunting ground for men more ruthless than the beast itself. The thrilling conclusion to the Wolves of Kalinin duology.

The Seven Deaths Of Prince Vlad

For lovers of A House with Good Bones, Vampires of El Norte, Our Share of the Night, and The Boatman's Daughter, The Seven Deaths of Prince Vlad is a literary ode to the Gothic terror and action of Hammer Films.

History is penned by the victors—and the legend of Dracula was the lie Van Helsing needed the world to believe.

They Come When You Sleep

Sixteen terrifying tales of folk horror and the supernatural.

Legend Of Deer Woman & Other Tales

The 2024 Second Place Bookfest Award Winner in the category of Supernatural Fiction - Magic, Legends, & Lore.

Made in the USA
Coppell, TX
27 January 2026

69179926R10079